Readers love Andrew Grey

A Taste of Love

"…an emotional story that will have you in tears one minute, smiling and laughing the next."

—Love Romances & More

A Serving of Love

"…a compelling tale of two men who meet under less than favorable conditions and find something that is well worth the effort."

—Sensual Reads

Dutch Treat

"The emotional pull was strong and the story was great It was definitely worth reading, and will become a permanent addition to my library for sure."

—Long and Short Reviews (formerly Whipped Cream Reviews)

Positive Resistance

"With the right amount of suspense, sizzle and a burgeoning romance between two people, the readers are treated to a story that hits all the right spots in your heart."

—Love Romances & More

Love Means… No Fear

"I would recommend this story to anyone looking for romance. I also found this series to be a lovely introduction to m/m erotica."

—The Romance Studio

http://www.dreamspinnerpress.com

A HELPING OF Love

ANDREW GREY

Dreamspinner Press

Published by
Dreamspinner Press
382 NE 191st Street #88329
Miami, FL 33179-3899, USA
http://www.dreamspinnerpress.com/

A Helping of Love
Copyright © 2012 by Andrew Grey

Cover Art by Reese Dante   http://www.reesedante.com

ISBN: 978-1-61372-392-0

Printed in the United States of America
First Edition
March 2012

eBook edition available
eBook ISBN: 978-1-61372-393-7

To Amy Lane, Mary Calmes, Connie Bailey, Ariel Tachna, Madeleine Urban, Rhianne Aile, and so many other authors who have all been an inspiration to me.
Thank you.

CHAPTER ONE

"DO YOU think you'll have the time to call on a potential new client today?" Annette asked through the speakerphone as Peter ate his breakfast cereal. "Jerry's been trying to get Café Belgie's business for almost a year now, and they actually gave him a call. He figures he'll only get this one chance, and it would make his day if we could get them as clients. He might even be willing to cough up a bonus."

Peter coughed and nearly sprayed half-chewed Grapenuts all over his table before he managed to swallow. "Pigs don't fly," Peter replied with laughter, and he heard Annette's devious laugh through the speaker. "He's the cheapest bastard I know, and that's probably why he already has more money than I'll ever see in my lifetime."

"Me too," Annette chimed in. Picking on Jerry was a pastime for both of them, and Jerry sometimes made it so easy. "So I can tell Jerry you'll do it?"

"Sure. Could you call and reschedule some of my morning appointments? Tell Jerry I'll stop by Café Belgie late this morning, and remind him that he owes me. And you too, for that matter."

"I won't let him forget," Annette told him, and Peter had no doubt Annette would hold this favor over Jerry until he coughed up something, maybe even a lung. That woman was tenacious in the best way possible as far as Peter was concerned. "Have a good day and be careful. They're calling for heavy rain today." Annette hung up, and Peter pressed the disconnect button on the phone. He finished his breakfast, placing his silverware and glass in the bowl before setting it on his lap and wheeling himself over to the sink. After rinsing the items off, Peter placed them in the dishwasher, looking around the room to make sure everything was clean. Once he was satisfied he hadn't forgotten anything, Peter wheeled himself to his bedroom and over to the closet, where he picked out a dress shirt and tie. Peter had learned a while ago not to put his shirt on before breakfast. He had a habit of spilling on it or getting it wet when he leaned over to work at the sink. Since it was summer and humid as all get-out, he decided to forego a jacket, and after checking himself in the mirror, he left the bedroom.

Peter double-checked that he had all his client information in his bag and fastened it onto his chair. Gliding through the ranch-style house, Peter made sure everything was locked up before wheeling himself to the back door and out into his garage. Locking the door behind him, he carefully made his way down the short ramp to the driver's side of his car. Peter opened his car door, getting his chair into position so he could slide into the driver's seat. Over the years, he'd gotten very good at taking care of himself, and after he was in place, Peter folded up the chair, maneuvering it behind his seat. He pressed a button and the back door closed. Peter pulled his own door closed before pressing the button to open the garage door and backing the car out.

Rain pelted the windshield as soon as he cleared the garage, and Peter groaned at the thought of getting around in this downpour, but it couldn't be helped. Reaching up to the visor, Peter pressed the button to lower the garage door and drove to his first appointment. Thankfully they had an awning out front, and Peter was able to get inside without getting too wet. After meeting with the restaurant owner, Peter left with a good-sized order for all-new fine restaurant china and flatware. "Thank you," Peter said at the doorway of the restaurant, shaking the restaurateur's hand. "Call me if you need anything, and I'll stop by in a few months otherwise."

"Of course," Ian said with a smile and sparkling eyes. Peter knew Ian was gay, and he tried not to let himself read anything into the expression. The man was drop-dead gorgeous. Ian's Pastiche restaurant had been a good customer for Peter ever since he'd gotten this job three years ago, and if the truth be known, Peter had had a slight crush on the man since he'd first met him. However, their relationship was strictly professional. Once, about a year ago, Peter had tried to move their relationship to a more personal level, but Ian had shown no interest.

Peter had gotten used to that. But just because he was in a wheelchair, that did not mean everything below the waist had stopped working. Peter had found out quickly after his accident that very few people he met ever looked beyond the wheelchair to actually see him, and those who did, never seemed to think of him in any sort of sexual way or as someone they might consider a relationship with. Not that Peter could necessarily blame them. Building a life with someone who couldn't walk would be a difficult proposition for most people. Hell, it had been a difficult proposition for Peter when he'd first found out he would never walk again. But he was a survivor, and he made the best of his situation.

Ian held the front door of the restaurant open, and Peter wheeled himself outside, thankful that the rain had nearly stopped and that there weren't any stairs to contend with. Peter got himself in the car and began the ten-mile drive from Mechanicsburg to Carlisle and Café Belgie.

The rain began again as he got close to the historic town, and by the time he parked in front of the Belgian restaurant, the rain was coming down in sheets. Peter decided to wait it out. Reaching around the seat, he pulled his bag onto his lap and began doing paperwork until the air in the car got so steamy he couldn't stand it anymore. Thankfully, the rain appeared to let up again, and Peter used what was probably only a temporary respite to get himself out of the car and down to the street corner where there was a ramp so he could get onto the sidewalk.

The sky opened up as Peter made his way down the uneven sidewalk. He picked up his pace so he wouldn't get totally soaked. Looking up, he saw a man hurrying in his direction carrying a huge umbrella. To Peter's relief, he stopped next to him. "Let me help you," the man said, and to Peter's surprise, he didn't try to take control of the chair the way most people did. Instead, he stood next to Peter and held the umbrella over both of them. "Are you Peter from Gold Restaurant Supply? Darryl said you were coming and asked me to watch for you because you were in a wheelchair." The man gasped and clamped his hand over his mouth. "Sorry."

"Why?" Peter shrugged. "I am in a wheelchair."

"It's not polite," the man responded, embarrassed, and Peter stole a look up at him, watching his face turn beet red.

"Most people don't talk about my chair. But then, most people ignore the chair and me along with it. So don't be embarrassed, and you weren't impolite." Peter smiled before continuing toward the front door of the restaurant. The man opened the door, and Peter wheeled himself inside the restaurant, pleased to be out of the rain. As he always did when he entered a new restaurant, Peter took in the surroundings so he could get an idea of what they might need. But Café Belgie had Peter stumped. Every table was impeccably set with bright, clean tablecloths. The dishes he could see looked nearly new, and even the floors were clean enough to eat off of.

"Are you Peter?" A tall man in a chef's uniform came out of the kitchen, crossing the dining room in huge strides. "I'm Darryl Hansen."

"Peter Christopoulos," he responded, and they shook hands. "This is a beautiful dining room," he complimented, once again looking around the space.

"Thanks," Darryl said with a smile. "You have to be wondering why we called you." Darryl motioned Peter to a table in back, and Peter noticed that one of the chairs had been removed. Peter took that place, and Darryl took one of the other places while the man who'd helped him with the umbrella sat across from him. "Before I forget, this is Russell Baker. He's going to be the chef of our new restaurant."

"Please call me Russ," was added in a soft voice, and Peter found himself smiling at him before turning back to Darryl.

"I have half an hour before we open for lunch, so if it's okay, I'd like to get right to business," Darryl prompted. "I called you because Jerry has been pestering me for a year to give his company a try. We're opening a new restaurant on Pomfret Street here in town, and the quote I got from our usual supplier was astronomical, so I decided to see if you could do better for us."

"I'll certainly try," Peter said, turning around to pull his bag off the handles of the chair. "What sort of restaurant are you opening? Do you need the standard equipment or something special?"

"My partner, Billy, and I were in Chicago a few months ago and found all of these small restaurants and stands selling gyros and other Greek food. We loved them, and when we got back, he tried to find a place like that here, but everyone makes a gyro with preformed patties, which are disgusting. We've decided to open a Greek restaurant, and Russ is going to be the chef and general manager."

"I know exactly what you mean," Peter said excitedly. "They roast the meat on a vertical roasting spit, and it cooks as it's needed."

"Exactly. We'll also have Greek salads, souvlaki, spanakopita, moussaka, and of course baklava. We've developed and tested the menu here with some of our loyal customers, and we believe we have the recipes down, so now we need an estimate on the equipment as well as installation," Darryl explained.

"The issue is that the space is small," Russ continued, his voice barely carrying across the table, and for a second Peter wondered how he could survive in a kitchen and be heard over the din. "So we have a tight budget for furnishing the restaurant in order to keep overhead under control." Russ stood up and moved to the chair next to him, pulling a small notebook out of his pocket. "Here's a list of the things we feel we'll need, along with an approximate cost estimate, as well as the space allotted in the kitchen."

Peter looked over the list and their budget, thinking for a second. "Are you making standard frozen French fries?"

Both Darryl and Russ looked appalled. "Absolutely not. The fries will be fresh," Darryl answered. "It'll be a variation on the recipe we use here, except with a slight seasoning to give the fries a kick."

Peter nodded and continued looking over the list. "I think I have some ideas for you. I assume you are not opposed to used equipment as long as it's in good condition and clean. The vertical gyros grills will need to be new, but I believe I can get much of the other equipment for you at a good price." Peter looked at Darryl and then at Russ. Both men seemed pleased.

"I have to get ready for lunch service," Darryl said as he stood up. "You can work out any details with Russ, and once you have a proposal, the two of you can run it by me for my approval." Darryl shook his hand and left the dining room.

"I really think I can make this happen within your budget," Peter supplied.

"Cool." Russ's face lit with excitement, and Peter couldn't help smiling in return.

"I'm pretty excited myself. With a last name like Christopoulos, it would be nice to finally have a place to get good Greek food. Since my mother passed away a few years ago, I haven't had much good home cooking. Maybe you could try your recipes out on me?" *Where did that come from? God, am I actually flirting with Russ?*

Russ smiled, and for a second Peter saw pleasure and interest in Russ's eyes, something Peter hadn't seen in a while, but it quickly faded, and his expression turned wary and fearful. "I usually try out all my recipes on my boyfriend Barry," Russ explained, smiling slightly.

Peter felt like a bit of an idiot and tried not to let it show on his face. For a second he'd thought that smile on Russ's face might have been for him, but it was just Russ's general excitement about the restaurant. He should have known better. No one ever saw him that way. "Would you like to see the restaurant?" Russ asked, pulling him out of his thoughts. "It's stopped raining, and that way you could see the space."

Russ sounded so excited that Peter shrugged off his discomfort. "Sure. That would be helpful. Is the location accessible?" In older towns like Carlisle, some of the stores still had stairs, and while new businesses had to be accessible, some of the older buildings had yet to be converted.

"There aren't any stairs," Russ said before giving Peter the address.

"Good. Then I'll meet you there." Peter wheeled himself toward the front door as the restaurant was opening for business, and after saying goodbye and thanking the waiter who opened the door for him, Peter glided down the sidewalk and then back up to his car.

The clouds were still very low and heavy as he pulled up in front of the building that would house the new restaurant. Peter was almost reluctant to get out of the car, but he was curious, and seeing the kitchen would help him make sure he got the right equipment for his customers. Opening the car door, he transferred himself to the chair as quickly as he could, making his way to the front. Russ opened the door, and Peter glided inside.

"As you can see, we still have some work to do out here, but the dining room is beginning to come together," Russ explained as he led Peter toward the back. "Darryl and Billy brought back pictures of some of the places they ate at, but they were diners with Formica tables and old booths for seating. We wanted to take it upscale just a little and make the food authentic." Russ held the door, and Peter rolled into what would be the kitchen. "At Café Belgie, the average bill is approximately $25 to $40 a diner, where here at the Acropolis, we expect the average check to be $12 to $18 a diner. That's the reason for the need to keep the overhead low, so we can still keep the food quality where it needs to be."

Peter listened as he looked around the space, envisioning where all the equipment, prep tables, and workstations would be. "Have you been working in restaurants long?" Peter asked as he continued to build the picture in his mind.

"A few years. I started out as a server and then moved into the kitchen as a prep cook before getting promoted to line cook. I've sort of done it all. Darryl is giving me a chance to do what I've always wanted, to run an entire restaurant, and I don't want to let him down."

A crack of thunder brought Peter's thoughts back to more immediate concerns. "I appreciate you showing me the space, but I should get back to the car before the sky opens up again. I'll see what I can put together, and I should be in touch with an estimate by the end of the week." Peter glided through the empty restaurant space, and Russ hurried past him, holding open the front door. Peter wheeled outside to the driver's door of his car just as the sky opened up like someone had turned on a faucet. Pushing the button on his key, Peter opened the driver's door and hurried to slide himself into the seat and get his chair in the back before it was completely soaked.

"I'll get the chair for you," Russ said, and Peter saw him pull his bag off the handles, placing it on the back seat. Peter lifted himself with his arms, transferring himself to the driver's seat. Lightning flashed and thunder vibrated around him. Peter tried to hurry, and the chair moved from under him. Grabbing for the steering wheel, he got a grip and held on, hanging out of the car, legs he had little control over sliding under the car. He tried to pull himself up, but his legs caught between the car and the curb and Peter couldn't pull them out. "It's okay, I have you," Russ said near his ear, and Peter wanted to close his eyes and die of total embarrassment. Who cared that he was now drenched to the skin, the very thing he was trying to avoid by rushing.

Russ's arms around his waist tugged him up and away from the car. Using his arms, Peter was able to pull himself onto the seat in a sopping wet, mortified mess. "Thank you," Peter said and turned toward Russ, trying his very best to be gracious rather than doing what he wanted, which was to close the door, drive away, and never see Russ again for as long as he lived. Peter fought a constant battle for his independence, and this only served as a reminder that no matter how much he tried, he was still dependent on others.

"Are you all right?" Russ asked, water running down his face, black hair plastered to his head.

"Yes," Peter responded breathlessly. Peter turned toward Russ to thank him again, and he gasped before he could stop himself. "What happened to your arm? Did I do that?" Russ's shirtsleeve had ridden up, and Peter saw black-and-blue marks going up Russ's arm that looked nasty and painful. That couldn't have just happened.

Russ yanked his sleeve down his arm. "I fell at the house the other day and tried to catch myself." Russ stepped away from the car. "I'll talk to you later in the week." Peter could tell Russ was trying to keep his voice light to cover up something. He knew, because it was the same tone he'd used in physical therapy when he was hurting like hell and didn't want the therapist to know. Russ closed Peter's car door and waved before hurrying into the restaurant. Sopping wet, Peter used the Bluetooth connection in his car to call Annette.

"I'm heading home," he told her once she answered. "I got caught in the rain, and I'm soaked." He left out the totally embarrassing part. "Could you please call my appointments and tell them I'm running late?"

"Of course, hon. How did it go at Café Belgie?"

"I think I can get the business if I can get some good used equipment. I already know we have some of the things they need." He rattled off the things he could remember. "And I'll check into the others. I'll forward the bid tonight, and you can do your magic. They already have a quote from their regular supplier. If we can beat it, the business is ours, and Jerry will completely platz." At least that made up for squishy underwear.

"I'll look for it in the morning. Get dry and call if you need anything."

Peter promised he would and hurried home as fast as the weather would allow. Once he arrived, he spent nearly an hour getting out of his wet clothes, drying off, and getting into dry things. He also dried off his wet chair and got on the road again. Thankfully, the rest of his day went better, and by the time he'd made all his calls, the skies had cleared. Peter decided he needed some exercise, so he stopped at home to change and get a different chair. He drove to the local high school and parked near the running track, getting out his chair—this one sleek and sturdy, custom made for him. Peter slid into it and wheeled himself toward the running surface.

Getting into position, he began moving forward, his arms propelling the wheels on the racing chair. As he picked up speed, his chest, shoulders, and back came into play, and he zoomed around the banked oval. The chair was weighted for him and could turn on a dime. As he picked up speed, Peter's blood raced through his body, heart pumping life through him. After a while, it felt as though he were flying around the oval, arms and chest throbbing, letting him know they were being worked. He passed a runner in a blur and continued moving, staying in one of the middle lanes, out of the way.

Peter kept moving, passing a few more runners and staying in the groove. Breathing through his nose and mouth, he reveled in the exercise, trying not to think about how he'd been before a drunk driver changed his life forever. But that was a while ago, and Peter pushed it away. It wasn't hard, not out here in the evening air, passing runners like they were standing still. Twenty minutes, half an hour, forty-five minutes, each milestone passed with a small beep of his watch. Once he reached his goal, he slowed but continued moving to cool off. "Hey, dude, that was cool," one of the runners called as he caught up with Peter, running as Peter kept pace with them.

"Thanks," Peter said with a smile.

"Do you compete?" a familiar voice asked, and Peter glanced to the side to see Russ running along with the other guys.

"I want to, but I'm not sure I'm good enough yet," Peter answered truthfully.

"I'd say you were. You looked like you were flying," Russ told him, and as Peter slowed, he noticed that Russ did as well, the other guys getting ahead of them. "When I saw you, I wanted to make sure you were okay. I didn't hurt your legs, did I?"

Peter shook his head. "I have a slight bruise, not from you, but nothing worse than that. It'll heal in time, but I have to keep an eye on it. How's your arm? Does it hurt?" Peter noticed that Russ was wearing a pressure bandage on each arm to cover his wrists.

"No," Russ said, touching one of his wrists. "I'm a bit clumsy, I guess."

Peter didn't argue, and they came to a stop off to the side of the track. Russ was as covered in sweat as Peter, his white T-shirt almost translucent, small nipples almost visible.

"Russ, are you ready to go home?" a man called as he strode across the grass, dressed in what looked to Peter to be a tailored suit.

"Almost," he answered before turning back to Peter. "I'll talk to you later in the week, and I think you're good enough to compete." Russ smiled before turning and walking toward the man who Peter assumed was Barry. The large man looked impatient, and as Russ approached, Barry hustled him toward a white Corvette, where Barry appeared to throw a shirt at Russ, obviously afraid to get the seat of his "compensating for my small penis" sports car dirty. Curious, Peter watched Russ strip off his shirt, and he stifled a gasp at what looked like black-and-blue marks on Russ's shoulder.

"The man's an asshole," one of the runners said from behind Peter. "If he got anywhere near me, I'd shove that Corvette up his ass." Peter laughed at the other man's joke and looked away after Russ pulled on the fresh shirt and got into the car. Barry started the engine, revving it as loudly as he could before pulling out, tires squealing.

Peter rarely hated someone on sight, but Barry fell into that category. His very demeanor screamed self-righteous, sanctimonious asshole. Well, that was none of Peter's business. Russ seemed like a really nice guy, but he was taken. Not that he'd looked at Peter twice. No one seemed to. "You like him," the kid next to him said. "It's okay, dude, I like guys too."

Peter turned away from watching where Russ and Barry had left. "Do you know Russ well?" Why couldn't he stop thinking about Russ? He had someone already.

"Not really. He runs with us sometimes. The big dude always picks him up and acts like a superior asshole, but Russ is cool, always nice, if a bit quiet." The kid said goodbye and walked back to where his friends had gathered, still recovering from their run. Peter held up his hand to the group, and they returned the gesture before turning as a group and walking across to the far side of the oval. Peter rolled to his car and drove home. He'd had a profitable day business-wise, but once again he was coming home to an empty house.

After his accident, Peter had lived with his parents, but he could see the burden of taking care of him was falling to his mother. And as her health deteriorated, Peter fought hard and long to become more and more independent. He got a job, bought himself a small house, and moved out on his own. Both his parents worried about him, but Peter needed to be self-sufficient. Before the accident, Peter had been an athlete, a track star with high hopes and dreams. All that ended when he'd opened his eyes in the hospital, unable to move his legs. Peter hadn't given up, and he'd channeled his athletic discipline and drive into his recovery. When it became evident there was no hope for him to walk again, he threw himself into becoming as independent as possible. That independence had come with a price, and living alone seemed to be it.

In his bedroom, Peter undressed and wheeled himself naked into the bathroom. After transferring himself to the toilet to take care of business, Peter wheeled himself into the shower, moving himself to the built-in seat using a series of bars.

The water felt heavenly, and Peter let it run over him before washing and using the hand-held sprayer to rinse himself. One of the things that had been hardest for him to get used to was the amount of time it took him to do almost everything. Activities he used to take for granted, such as a quick shower, now took time and a great deal of effort to accomplish. But he was doing it on his own, and he kept reminding himself that was a win. Turning off the water, Peter reached for the towel and realized he'd forgotten to place it on the hook before he got in the shower. Transferring himself back to the wheelchair, he opened the closet door and pulled out two towels and began drying both himself and his chair before moving into his bedroom to dress.

He made himself dinner, carrying his plate and utensils to the table on a tray he placed on his lap. As he ate, he began completing the proposal details for the Acropolis. Pushing his plate aside when he was done, Peter retrieved his laptop and began sending order and proposal details to Annette. He'd just finished when his phone rang.

"Hi, Dad," Peter said cheerfully. "How are you?"

"I'm okay," his father answered, sounding down. "I've been cleaning out more stuff from the house, and I came across some things your mother had wanted you to have. I'll give them to you when you come over this weekend."

"Okay," Peter answered, concerned about the way his father sounded. "What's going on?" His father had been on a kick to clean out the house lately. Peter knew part of it was his father finally moving on, but he was curious why now.

"I've made some decisions, and I don't want you to be angry. I'm going to sell the house and move into assisted living. It's getting harder for me to keep up with things. Some friends of your mother's and mine have moved into Luther Manor, and they seem to like it." His dad sounded unsure, but Peter felt relief more than anything.

"That's good," Peter told his dad. "You won't have lawn to mow and a house to take care of. Can you still keep your car?"

"Yes, and I'll have my own one-bedroom apartment." The relief in his dad's voice rang through the line. "I thought you'd be mad at me for selling your mother's house." That was how his dad always thought of the house Peter had grown up in. They hadn't had a lot of money, but Peter's mom had worked with her own brand of energy and motherly magic to create a home filled with love. Peter missed her each and every day.

"Not at all, Dad. Do you need help going through things?"

"No. I've already been through most everything, but we can talk about anything you'd like this weekend. The house will go on the market next month, and I'm scheduled to move into my apartment in October."

Peter's head swam. He hadn't expected his father to move so fast or to do all this without talking it over with him. "Isn't this kind of sudden?" Peter swallowed hard, because he didn't want to come off sounding like a dick.

"Kind of." Peter's dad sounded unsure again, and Peter cringed; he knew he had to be positive. "I applied, and they had an unexpected opening, so I took it."

"Good. You'll be in by winter and won't have to worry about having snow to shovel or slippery sidewalks." Yes, this was a bit of a surprise, but it would be good for his dad. Peter had offered to have his dad move in with him, but that had problems of its own. In assisted living, Peter knew there would be people to look after his dad in ways that he couldn't. Their conversation turned to more normal subjects, and they got caught up with each other. After talking for nearly half an hour, they said good night, and Peter went back to work. Once his paperwork was done, Peter went into the living room and watched television for an hour until it was time for bed.

Peter brushed his teeth and went to the bedroom, sliding himself from his chair to the bed. After making sure the chair was in its place, should he need it, Peter turned out the lights, but couldn't fall asleep. He thought about turning on his small bedroom television to watch his favorite video, but decided against it and instead rolled onto his side. Just because his legs no longer worked, didn't mean his heart didn't, or that other parts of his anatomy weren't just as vital and healthy as the next man's. But all he'd had was his hand for three years, and he wanted more. "I'm tired of being invisible." Peter couldn't get comfortable and continued to toss in the bed. Finally, he lifted his body, shoving pillows under his back so he could sit up. Reaching to the nightstand, he grabbed the book he'd been reading. When he'd bought it, he hadn't realized it was a romance, and the ending left him both happy for the characters and sad, because he wanted what they had, but Peter wasn't sure that was even a possibility for him.

CHAPTER TWO

RUSS rolled over and away from Barry, trying to find a comfortable position. "Would you stop moving? I'm trying to sleep," Barry growled softly, punching his pillow before rolling over so violently Russ bounced on the mattress. "You always do that, and I have a big day tomorrow."

Russ slid out from between the covers and grabbed his pillow, walking into the office, where he lay down on the sofa, pulling a blanket over himself. Russ used to hope that Barry would be sorry that he wasn't sleeping next to him, but Barry never came to get him and rarely if ever even mentioned that Russ had spent the night on the sofa. Rolling over, Russ hissed softly to himself when he lay wrong, his side a little tender. Shifting and finally getting comfortable, he could hear Barry snoring loudly in the other room, so he got up and closed the door to block out the sound. Russ lay back down and finally went to sleep.

When he woke, the house was quiet. The door to the office stood open, but Russ couldn't hear any movement. Checking the time, Russ jumped up and hurried to the bedroom. He was late for work already, and Barry hadn't bothered to wake him up. Picking up the phone, he called the restaurant, and Billy, Darryl's partner, answered. "We were getting a little worried."

"I overslept," Russ explained, mortified that he was letting them down.

"It's fine. Get here when you can, and I'll tell Darryl. Don't worry about it," Billy added, but Russ did worry about it. He liked his job, and Darryl was giving him a chance that Russ wasn't sure he completely deserved, but he was determined to make good on it regardless.

"Thanks. I'm going to clean up, and I'll be right in." Russ hung up the phone and rushed to the bathroom, stripping off the underwear and T-shirt he'd slept in before turning on the water. He showered quickly, resisting the urge to take the time to let the hot water soothe his aching back. Turning off the water, Russ stepped out and dried himself off before refolding his towel and hanging it on his towel rod. Then he picked up the bath mat, hanging it up as well. Finally, he gave the room one more look before walking back into the bedroom. Opening his drawer, Russ took a meticulously folded pair of underwear and a set of perfectly matched socks from his drawer before closing it, lining the bottom of the drawer up with the others. He almost sat on the edge of the bed, but stopped himself or he'd have to remake it so Barry wouldn't be cross with him. Instead, he remained standing as he pulled them on. Walking to his closet, Russ stopped in front of the mirrored door. Russ looked behind him, almost expecting to see someone with him as a stranger stared back at him.

Russ knew it was him, but he looked thin, his face pale. The bruises on his wrists had nearly faded, but a new one was darkening on his side. Opening the closet door, he carefully pulled out a white shirt from among the others, all hung in their color families. Putting on the shirt, Russ made sure it covered his wrists before removing a pair of jeans from their hanger. He knew he'd change into his chef clothes at work, but the need to look nearly perfect was so ingrained, he barely thought about it now. Russ finished dressing before closing the closet doors, making sure they latched and nothing stuck out. He then looked around the immaculate bedroom for anything out of place before descending the stairs. Taking his wallet and keys from their place in the bowl by the door, Russ hurried to his car and drove in to work.

"I'm really sorry for being late," he told Darryl as soon as he walked into the kitchen and took his place near his boss, who was already getting ready for lunch.

"We had your back," Darryl said, but Russ felt his boss's eyes slide over him, appraising him. "It's happened to all of us. Go on and change. After lunch, Peter from Gold's Food Service Equipment is meeting with us to go over the equipment quotes." Darryl continued looking at him, and Russ couldn't help feeling there was something else he wanted to say. Russ turned away and hurried toward the back to change his clothes so he could get to work.

Thankfully, he didn't have a lot of time to think about anything other than his work until lunch was over, but both Darryl and Billy watched him curiously whenever they saw him, and Russ didn't quite know what to make of it. Maybe Darryl had changed his mind and had decided to find someone else to run the new restaurant, and they were trying to figure out how to tell him. Russ quivered at the thought, checking to make sure no one had seen him. At the end of service, Darryl whipped up lunch for everyone, and they gathered at the traditional staff lunch table in the dining room.

Russ carried in a large bowl of pesto and sat at what he'd come to think of as his place. Billy sat next to Darryl, with the front of house manager, Sebastian, across from Russ. The other staff joined them, and everyone talked as the food got passed around the table. Soon they were joined by Davey and Donnie, Billy's twin brothers. They didn't seem hungry, but they sat around the table as well. In the time he'd worked at Café Belgie, Russ had learned that the staff lunch was a family meal in almost every sense of the word. "Any ideas for specials?" Darryl asked over the din of conversation and food. Ideas were often thrown out and discussed frankly and openly.

"I have an idea for the new restaurant," Russ interjected into the conversation. "It's an eggplant dish, though I'm not sure how it will be received."

"Make some up tomorrow, and we'll try it out at lunch. If it works, we'll use it as a special and add it to the menu at the

Acropolis." Darryl smiled and nodded encouragingly at him, and Russ returned to his food.

The dishes were being carried away when Russ heard a knock on the front door and saw Peter sitting in his chair outside. Russ tried to push away his thoughts regarding how handsome and nice he thought Peter was. He had the most amazing dark eyes, rich olive skin, and the face of a Hollywood model with what looked like shiny, soft, jet-black hair that almost reached his collar. The man was sexy, without a doubt. Russ shook his head slightly to clear the thoughts as he walked toward the front door. He could not think like that. Barry had gone ballistic when he'd seen Russ talking to Peter at the track, and somehow Barry always seemed to know if Russ looked at anyone for too long. "Come on in," Russ said as he opened the door, suppressing a twinge of excitement when Peter looked up at him. "We're just finishing up. Would you like something to drink?"

"Coffee would be nice," Peter answered with a smile.

"I'll get it," Billy said from behind, lightly touching him on the shoulder. "Darryl will be right out." Billy went to the servers' station, and Russ led Peter toward the table. Russ pulled back one of the chairs, letting Peter wheel himself to the table. Russ sat down, and Darryl joined them a few minutes later as Billy brought over coffee cups, sitting down as well. "Davey and Donnie are watching television in the back."

Peter removed his bag from the back of his chair. "I think I was able to get almost everything you need used. A restaurant in Harrisburg closed a few weeks ago, and we bought the contents of their kitchen. They hadn't been open for very long, so all their equipment was less than a year old," Peter explained as he handed each of them copies of the proposal. "As you can see, I was able to bring all the equipment in at about $12,000 under your budget."

Russ stared at the numbers and then looked up at Darryl, who appeared to be beaming. "This is amazing," Darryl murmured.

"The only equipment I couldn't get used was the upright grills, but they're a specialty item. I can order them from a Chicago company to make sure you get the authentic equipment, but there is a problem." Peter fished around in his bag. "The meat they use is locally produced, and the closest supplier I can find is in New York, but the ingredients aren't quite the same." Peter handed Darryl a sheet on printer paper. "This is the name of the company that sells the grills. They also have the contacts regarding the lamb and beef gyros meat. I wasn't sure if you'd lined up a supplier, so I thought I'd pass on the information." Peter looked almost as excited as Russ felt. It really looked like the restaurant was coming together.

"How soon can we get the equipment?" Darryl asked with a grin.

"I reserved the used equipment in our warehouse, so once I get the signed order and a check, I'll arrange delivery and installation as well as place the order for the remaining equipment. When were you planning to open?"

"Two months," Russ answered excitedly. That had been their original plan, but when their first estimate had come in so high, Russ had been afraid they might need to delay.

"That shouldn't be a problem," Peter said with a smile before lifting his coffee cup to his lips.

"You're a miracle worker," Russ said, and Peter smiled, coloring slightly under his rich olive cheeks.

"I'll call the bank today and arrange for a check to go out tomorrow," Darryl said. "Now, with the money you saved us, let's talk about the rest of the furnishings we'll need." They got down to business, and by the time Peter got ready to leave, Darryl had signed the purchase order for the equipment and they had decided on the dishes, utensils, as well as pots and pans for the kitchen—almost everything they needed, even the tablecloths and napkins.

"Thank you," Peter said with a smile as he took the signed papers. "I'll get all the orders placed tonight, and equipment should begin arriving late next week. I'll stop by the Acropolis to make sure everything is delivered properly, and then I can arrange for installation." Peter shook hands with Darryl and Billy before pushing himself back from the table.

"I'll walk you out," Russ offered, striding to the front door, holding it for Peter. "Thank you so much." Russ held out his hand, and Peter took it. Russ was surprised at the firm roughness in the other man's grip, as well as the fact that Russ didn't want to release Peter's hand. "Thank you," Russ said after letting go and looking at the floor.

"You're welcome," Peter answered before gliding out the door and down the sidewalk. Russ watched him go, standing in the doorway until Peter reached his car. Then he stepped back inside and closed the door. When he turned around, Russ saw Darryl and Billy staring at him.

"I think we need to talk," Darryl said and motioned with his head toward the kitchen. Russ followed, not at all sure what was going on, but his stomach began to churn.

"Would you two go out front?" Russ heard Billy say to his brothers, and they filed past, carrying their handheld video games. They knew something was wrong—Russ could tell by the way they looked at him. Once he was in the office, Billy shut the door behind them.

"Russ, sit down," Darryl said softly. "Billy and I have meant to talk to you for some time, but we didn't know what to say, and we thought we could be wrong, but now we don't think so."

"What have I done?"

"You haven't done anything," Billy said, sitting next to him. "But we know that Barry has been abusing you. We've seen the marks on your wrists, and I know you're hurting because you've been favoring your right side all day."

"Barry hasn't done anything. I've been clumsy and hurt myself." The lie rolled off his tongue so naturally he almost believed it. But he couldn't let them know how weak he was or what he'd done wrong.

"You're never clumsy. In all the time you've worked here, you've never so much as dropped a dish. Whatever Barry's got you thinking, or made you think, we know what he's doing. We've seen it and we've seen the way he treats you," Darryl told him as he leaned closer. "You're our friend as well as a great employee. We hate to see you being hurt."

Russ didn't know what to say as the walls he'd built around himself to insulate his mind from the hurt began to crumble. "It isn't Barry's fault. It's mine. I'm the one who's always doing things wrong." Russ began to shake as he thought of how Barry would react if he were here, the fear overwhelming him, blackness beginning to form around the edge of his vision.

"What did you do last night to make Barry angry enough to hit you in the side?" Billy asked, and Russ felt as well as saw him looking into his eyes. He had to turn away, putting his hands over his face to hide himself and his shame. He felt hands touch his shoulders, and Russ shrugged them away, but they returned, more insistently, until he was being hugged. "It's okay. None of this is your fault."

"It's all my fault! You don't understand. Everything is my fault!"

"That's Barry talking, trying to control you."

"But he loves me," Russ said softly.

Billy held him tighter as he lightly stroked his back. "I don't know what Barry feels, but it isn't love. If he loved you, he wouldn't hit you and try to control you. That's not love." Russ heard what Billy was saying, but all he could do was shake. It felt as though his whole world was crashing down around him, and he could do nothing to stop it. "We'll help you if you want it."

"Help me?" Russ said, lifting his head away from Billy as he tried to get himself under control. "I have nothing at all. Everything is Barry's. I don't even have a car. The one I drive belongs to Barry. No one can help me." Russ shot to his feet, moving toward the door. The small office suddenly felt stifling, and he had to get out, but as he approached, he saw Darryl standing in front of the door, arms crossed.

"We're doing this because we care for you. We want you to be happy, and you aren't now." Darryl stepped aside. "You can leave, but you're running because you're afraid. And aren't you tired of being afraid all the time?"

Russ stared at the door, not sure what he should do. Then he felt himself falling, his legs crumbling from under him. "Get him on the sofa," Billy said, and Russ felt himself being lifted and set down again. "You're okay. Breathe."

Russ tried to do what Billy asked, and after several attempts he managed to take a few shallow breaths that got easier and easier.

"You're going to be okay. We'll help you with whatever you decide," Billy comforted.

As soon as Russ could breathe, the tears he'd barely been able to hold at bay broke through, and he felt himself crying, turning away from Billy and Darryl so they wouldn't see him come apart. His embarrassment was complete, and he couldn't look at anyone. Then he felt a hand slide into his. "It's okay. Let everything out. You've held the pain inside for so long, you didn't know you were carrying it around. It's okay to let it go," Billy soothed, and Russ heard the door open and then close quietly. God, he hoped no one else saw him like this. When he looked, Russ saw that he and Billy were alone in the room.

What was he going to do? Russ's thoughts refused to settle on anything as he wiped his eyes and tried to stop his blubbering. But the tears and pain kept coming. "You don't deserve to be treated like that," Billy whispered into his ear.

"Yes, I do," Russ gasped, swallowing hard around the lump in his throat. "I allowed it to happen, so I must have deserved it." He buried his face back into the cushions, feeling completely helpless and alone. Yes, Billy was there with him, but on the inside, he was alone.

"You have a choice, Russ," Billy said softly. "Darryl was serious. He and I are here to support you because you're our friend and we care. You are not alone. Since you joined our family here, you've never been alone."

Russ sniffed and forced himself to turn away from the cushions, but he couldn't put words to everything that ran through his head. Where could he go? What did he really want to do? The thought of leaving Barry scared him to death, but the thought of staying scared him more.

"What happened last night?"

Russ clamped his eyes closed because he didn't want to think about it. But he knew Billy was not going to let it go. "It was my day off, so I joined Barry at the gym. I was on the treadmill, and one of the guys who'd finished his workout was talking to me. He wasn't doing anything," Russ explained, and he sniffed again, trying to keep himself under control, but he didn't know how long he was going to be able to. "We were just talking. Barry stormed up to him, and the man said goodbye and moved away. Barry didn't say anything to me there, but when we got home, he accused me of flirting with him. He said I'd been making eyes and flirting with him." Russ tried to catch his breath and stopped talking. "I can't. Barry will kill me."

Billy held his hand. "I know this is hard for you. But you need to stop letting Barry control every portion of your life. He hurt you, and no one should ever do that."

"Barry yelled and screamed at me. He said, like he always does, that I'm his. Then he grabbed me hard, and I lost my balance and fell against the kitchen table."

"Is that how you hurt your side?"

Russ shook his head. "No. Barry pushed me onto the table and showed me who I belong to. He took me right there in the kitchen, his hands digging into my flesh. He's always like that when he thinks someone else might have looked at me. He gets so jealous sometimes, and maybe I lead other guys on like he says. I don't mean to, but what if I'm doing it without knowing I am?" Russ grasped at any sort of explanation.

"You aren't. The problem is with Barry, not you. No matter what, you have a right to talk to people, and he does not have a right to hurt you." Billy became quiet for a while. "Did you like it when Barry did that to you?"

Russ became as still as death, his breath hitching as the expression on Barry's face played through Russ's mind. Barry hadn't kissed him or even looked happy. He'd been angry and almost possessed as he'd driven into Russ's body. There hadn't been any love or caring whatsoever. "I'm just another possession to him, like that stupid car or one of his suits." The realization hit Russ hard. Sitting up, he took measured deep breaths as some of the turmoil inside calmed. He seemed to be seeing more clearly as well. "I'm sorry." Russ swallowed hard before slowly getting to his feet.

"Do you need some time? I can go and you can stay in here for as long as you need." Billy didn't move away.

"I need some time to think," Russ said, standing up, checking his watch. "If it's okay, I'll be gone for about an hour."

Billy looked wary but smiled slightly. "Of course. But call if you need anything."

Russ opened the door, grabbing the small bag of extra clothes he kept with his work things. After changing clothes in the bathroom, Russ left by the back door and got into his car—correction, *Barry's car*—and drove to the track oval. After changing his shoes, Russ got out and slammed the car door as hard as he possibly could. Without turning back, he began to run. Faster and faster, he tried to outrace his thoughts to try to get his mind to calm, but they kept pace with him. "Fucking Barry," he muttered under his breath like a mantra, imagining each step stomping Barry further and further into the ground.

He vaguely saw someone zoom past him, but he barely noticed. His feet pounded the ground, lungs sucking air, and he kept moving, legs aching, but he continued pressing himself forward. Curve after curve passed behind him, and only when Russ felt his legs were about to give out from under him did he slow down to a walk, eventually coming to a stop before collapsing onto the grass. Russ didn't move or try to get up, and closed his eyes against the sun. The soft grass felt good on his back, and he continued breathing hard, his mind finally quiet, his anger and frustration spent for now.

"Are you okay, Russ?" Cracking his eyes open, he saw Peter's face above him. "Do you need help?"

"Yes… no," Russ answered, and he slowly lifted himself to a seated position. "Sorry, I'll be fine." Russ took another deep breath, his heart rate finally beginning to slow after the way he'd pushed his body.

"I've got some water," Peter said, and he handed Russ a large bottle. "Drink what you need."

Russ didn't think about it twice and drained almost every drop from the plastic container. "Thank you."

"You're welcome," Peter answered when Russ handed back the bottle. "Are you all right? You don't look so well." Russ sighed, finally allowing himself to look Peter in the face, and what he saw was something he hadn't seen in many people lately other than Billy and Darryl: genuine concern. The gentle softness in Peter's eyes went straight to Russ's heart, and he lowered his head, the tears threatening once again. "You're not okay," Peter said softly, and Russ shook his head.

"Do you need me to call someone?" Peter asked, but Russ couldn't answer. He could barely move, and it felt as though every ounce of energy had been wrung from his body. Russ tried to lift his head, but all he could see through watery eyes was Peter. He tried to answer, but he couldn't, and he let his body fall back onto the grass. His body and mind floated on wispy clouds, though in a way, he finally felt better, his thoughts no longer running in a million different directions.

"Russ!" he heard a familiar voice cry, and then he was being touched and caressed. "Russ, say something."

"I'm okay," he managed to answer.

"Drink," the voice said as someone lifted him up, and he complied automatically. Sweet liquid slid down his throat, and he continued drinking. "Take it easy."

Opening his eyes, Russ saw both Billy and Darryl along with Peter looking worriedly back at him. "I'm okay. I just overdid it." Russ breathed heavily and then drank some more from the bottle Billy held for him. The sweet liquid seemed to do the trick, and slowly he felt more and more like himself. "Thank you." Russ looked around. "How did you get here?" His mind seemed fuzzy, but was clearing.

"Peter called us," Darryl explained. "Can you stand up?"

"I think so," Russ answered before slowly getting to his feet. At first he felt wobbly, but his legs quickly steadied beneath him. "Thank you, Peter, for calling them." Russ took a few tentative steps toward Darryl's car before reaching it. Opening the back door, he climbed in and rested on the seat. His head still felt light and his legs ached. He'd have to come back and get his car later, but he really didn't care about that now.

"You could have hurt yourself," Billy scolded lightly as he got in the front seat. Russ nodded his head. He was just beginning to realize how far he'd pushed himself and what might have happened if Peter hadn't been there.

"I know. But I needed to clear my head, and I now know what I have to do," Russ explained. Sometime during his run, everything had become clear for him. "I'm going to leave." Russ knew this was going to be the hardest thing he'd ever done in his life. He had depended on Barry for years now, but that dependence was hurting him physically and emotionally.

"You're welcome to our guest room," Darryl explained as they stopped at a light. "We meant what we said about being there for you. It's going to take you some time to get back on your feet." Russ smiled and nodded, knowing what they said was true. "Do you want us to take you home so you can get your things?"

"No," Russ answered more sharply than he intended. "I need to do this myself."

Darryl parked in the lot in back of the restaurant, and they entered through the back door. Davey and Donnie looked up from where they sat on the sofa Russ had used earlier, their eyes big. "Are you okay, Uncle Russ?" Donnie asked. "You don't look so good."

"He's okay, Donnie," Billy said for him. "Have both of you read today?" Russ saw the boys set down their computer games, each reaching for a book from the table. "You can play your games again once you've spent some time reading."

"Go on and take care of what you have to," Darryl told him, placing a hand on Russ's shoulder. "Billy is going to be leaving with the boys soon, and he'll help you get set up at the house."

Sebastian came into the kitchen through the swinging door to the dining room. "Peter is out front. He's asking about Russ, and we need to get ready for dinner." Billy sighed and followed Sebastian into the dining room, while Russ made sure he looked okay before following. Peter sat near the front door, looking extremely agitated.

"I was worried and stopped by to make sure you were really okay." Peter's deep eyes gave Russ pause when he saw nothing but care and concern. A near-perfect stranger showed him more consideration than Barry, the man he'd been with for nearly four years.

"I will be, thanks to you," Russ said, but he didn't know quite how to adequately thank him. "I guess I overdid it."

Peter nodded his head. "I heard you swearing and almost shouting as you were running. You must have been trying to outrun something really bad. I used to do that before...." Peter's voice trailed off for a second, and then he said, "Before the accident."

"You were a runner?" Russ asked. He hadn't realized, but up until that second Russ had never considered that Peter hadn't always been in that wheelchair. My God, how difficult it must have been to be able to run and then have that taken away. "Sorry. That was a stupid question. I mean...."

"It's okay. I understand, I really do. People see the chair and sort of assume that I've always been in it. I used to be a track star and had dreams of going to the Olympics, but that ended."

"So now you're training to race in wheelchairs. That's pretty cool." Russ thought it was amazing to be able to pick yourself up like that and move on, realizing he was going to have a difficult time doing that same thing in his own life. They seemed to run out of things to say, and Peter moved toward the door.

"I'm glad you're okay," Peter said before pulling open the door and gliding outside. Closing the door, Russ walked back through the restaurant.

"I'm leaving for the day, and I can give you a ride back to your car," Billy offered, herding the boys out the back door. Russ grabbed his bag, following behind. Once everyone was all set in the car, Billy drove Russ back to the school, and Russ waved as they drove away. Somehow, without really knowing it, Russ had made friends. Standing in the sunshine outside the car, Russ gazed around him, seeing things for what seemed like the first time. He had made friends, good friends, in spite of Barry.

Russ used to have a large circle of close friends, but now as he looked back, he could see that once he'd met Barry, his life had become a smaller and smaller circle that revolved more and more around Barry. It had happened so slowly that Russ hadn't even noticed it. Now all those people had been squeezed out of his life, and he hadn't even realized why or how. Barry had taken all his attention and all his effort, and in the process, Russ had allowed Barry to take away nearly everyone until only he was left and Russ had to depend solely on him. Russ banged his hand on the roof of the car and then looked to make sure there wasn't a dent. "Screw you!" He yelled, banging his hand again.

After all, the damned car was Barry's old white Nissan Sentra, but you'd think it was the greatest car on Earth, the way Barry was so compulsive about how Russ had to take care of it. The bastard insisted on white cars and actually had Russ wash the damned thing inside and out every Saturday because he couldn't stand to see any dirt on it.

Making a fist, Russ banged the roof again as hard as he could. This time there was a dent, and Russ left it. "Fuck you, Barry!" Getting in the car, he started the engine and drove to the house.

Parking in the immaculate garage, Russ walked through the yard and into the house. Out of habit he almost took off his shoes. "Screw that." Stomping through the house, he left a trail of dirt on the carpet as he rushed upstairs. In the storage closet, Russ found two pieces of Barry's expensive Louis Vuitton luggage. Carrying them to the bedroom, he placed them on the floor, staring at the perfectly made bed before ripping the spread, blanket, and sheet off the top and hurling everything to the floor. Then he placed the suitcases on the bed and opened them. Russ worked quickly to fill them, leaving every drawer open, knowing it would grind against Barry's compulsive soul. Once he had his clothes packed, Russ took a quick shower, leaving the towels and bath mat wherever they fell. Dressing in a hurry, he carried the suitcases down to the car, placing them in the trunk. "Goodbye, Barry," he said out loud as he inserted the key into the back door, but then he stopped.

Going back inside, Russ marched up the stairs and into the bedroom. "You're a controlling piece of shit," he yelled before pulling open Barry's drawers, stirring the neatly folded contents of each one into a jumbled mess before closing the drawer again. "Now for the coup de grâce," he added out loud, and he pulled open the door to Barry's closet.

Ten minutes later, Russ left by the back door, locking it behind him. And as he passed through the backyard, got into the car, and pulled out of the garage, driving toward where Billy and Darryl lived, he felt free. For the first time in a long time, he could breathe. Screw Barry, he didn't need that bastard and all his anal ways. He had a chance to get away and make his own life, and he was going to make the most of it. He just wished he could see Barry's face when he got home. He imagined Barry's face when he saw the unmade bed. The first thing he'd do would be to yell for Russ, and when he didn't answer, Barry would remake the bed because he wouldn't be able to stand leaving it that way. The yelling would get louder by the time he walked into the bathroom. Barry would immediately pick up the towels and put everything in its place because, like the bed, the bathroom had to be just so. Then Barry would walk to his closet and open the door… Russ snickered with glee as he imagined the redness starting in Barry's neck, extending up his cheeks and then to his ears. He even imagined smoke and a cartoon whistle as Barry's compulsive brain short-circuited when he saw every piece of his usually neatly arranged clothing in a huge, jumbled pile on the floor without a hanger in sight. Okay, he knew he was being petty and vindictive, but screw it. Barry had used all his rules to control him for years. Everything always had to be just so.

Pulling into Carlisle, Russ wound through town before finding a parking space near where Billy and Darryl lived. As he walked up the sidewalk, he saw the front door open, and Billy rushed out, pulling him into a hug. "I thought you might have changed your mind."

"Nope. You and Darryl were right. He's a controlling bastard, and I needed to get away from him." Russ returned Billy's hug. "I feel like I can see again, like I've been living in the dark and someone just turned on the lights." Russ nearly laughed out loud. "I do need to get his car back, though."

"Do you mind if I check something?" Billy asked, and Russ nodded. Billy walked to the car, opening the passenger door and then the glove compartment. After a few minutes, he stood back up, grinning and waving a sheet of paper.

"What?" Russ wondered out loud.

"I don't know about everything else, but the car isn't Barry's," Billy said as he handed Russ a registration with his name on it. "Come on, let's go inside, and this evening we'll call a friend of ours and maybe he can help determine what else is yours."

As he walked back toward the door, the full gravity of what he'd done hit Russ all at once. He'd left Barry, burned his bridges, and was about to be dependent on his boss and his partner. What in the hell had he done? With each step, he nearly turned around and raced back toward the car. If he got to work right now, he could clean up the mess he'd made back at home and Barry wouldn't ever know.

"Let's bring in your bags, and I'll show you your room," Billy said.

Russ stopped and returned to the car, opening the trunk. Billy got one of the bags, and he took the other, following Billy across the street. At the front door, Russ stopped and looked back at the car, knowing this was his last chance to turn back. Holding his breath, Russ walked into the house, and Billy closed the door. Russ had so many questions running through his head, but he'd gotten out and away from the man hurting him and controlling his life. Billy and Darryl were supporting him. He wasn't sure how long he could stay here with them, but as Russ climbed the stairs behind Billy, he vowed to himself to get out on his own as soon as possible. He'd let himself exist under Barry's thumb for way too long, and while he was sure Billy and Darryl weren't like Barry at all, Russ knew he needed to be on his own and completely free as soon as possible.

CHAPTER THREE

PETER was running late, so he skipped breakfast and went right out the back door to his car. After shifting into the driver's seat, he got his chair behind him before driving as fast as he could to the future location of the Acropolis. He'd placed all the orders and arranged delivery right after receiving payment, and since most of the equipment was already in Gold's warehouse, Peter had been able to expedite delivery and take advantage of an opening in the installation schedule. He'd met with Darryl and Russ a little more than a week ago, and already they were getting things installed. Parking in the handicap space in front of the restaurant, Peter got out and saw Russ waiting for him at the door, looking very nervous. "The installers are already here and they aren't doing it right. I had to stop them from putting the grill on the wrong wall."

"I'm sorry," Peter said as he rolled to the door. "I sent over the plans we worked up. We'll get it fixed, I promise." Peter rolled inside and saw the three installers glaring at Russ. Pulling the plans out of his bag, Peter laid them on the table. "Did you get copies of the plans?" he asked the lead installer.

"Yes. But the grill is too big to fit where the plans say, so we have to move it."

Peter wheeled himself closer. "Did you call and get permission to move it, or did you make the decision on your own? Because I measured the grill and the location, and it fits to the inch. I suggest you bring in all the equipment and set every piece in its proper place before you install anything, just to make sure." Peter kept his voice level. He'd dealt with this crew before, and they knew Peter was usually right. He also noticed that none of them argued with him as they all hurried to do what he wanted.

"Wow," Russ said with a smile.

"They're men who think they know what's best, and they tend to be skeptical of the plans. I've worked to try to change that, but it takes time. I doubt they meant to upset you."

"I know." Peter saw Russ sigh. "It's been a… difficult week or so." Peter nodded, and their conversation tapered off as the men began carrying in the equipment, setting it where it was to be installed. Peter stayed out of the way, but where he could watch, making minor corrections, and once all the equipment was in, it fit exactly where the plans said it would. Once that issue was cleared up, the men covered the equipment, moving it out of the way before beginning the installation of the vent hoods.

"Are you feeling better? The last time I saw you, things weren't going so well." Peter tried not to pry, but he couldn't help noticing that while Russ was still a bit shy and nervous, he also seemed happier.

"Yes. I dumped Barry and moved out," Russ said frankly, and Peter felt his heart do a little jump before he could stop it.

"Did you find a new place?" Peter wanted to ask all kinds of questions.

"I'm staying with Billy and Darryl until I can find an apartment." Russ seemed wary, and Peter returned his attention to what the installers were doing. They seemed to have things well in hand for now, so Peter wheeled himself out into what would be the dining room, and he noticed that Russ followed him.

"Can I ask you something?" Peter inquired, and Russ nodded stiffly. "Was Barry the guy who picked you up at the track the first time I saw you there?"

"Yes, that was him."

"He was an asshole," Peter said before he could stop himself, and he clamped his lips closed, afraid he'd said too much.

It was a relief when he heard Russ's rich laugh. "Why is it that I was with him for four years, and you knew he was an asshole after seeing him from a distance?"

"I saw the way he tried to control you. He made you change your shirt before getting in the car, and he practically dragged you away like he owned you." Peter felt so serious, and he saw what looked like a dark cloud settle over Russ's face. "Besides, he drove a small-penis car, and any gay man who drives a car like that has to be an asshole to make up for his tiny ding-a-ling." Peter wagged his pinkie at Russ and smiled when the man laughed again, this time harder than before.

"You don't know the half of it." Russ wagged half a pinkie at Peter, and their laughter filled the empty space.

Once the laughter died down, Peter thought that now might be the time to take a chance. "Had Barry been hurting you? I saw the marks on your wrist, and when you changed your shirt by the car, I saw a large bruise on your shoulder."

"You were watching me?" Russ sounded frightened and took a step back.

"Well, yeah, I was watching." Peter lowered his voice. "You're very attractive, and I didn't like the way Barry acted around you. He looked at you like the thought of him waiting a few minutes while you talked to me was about as appealing as dog crap on his shoes."

"You got all that from just seeing him?" Russ asked, and it looked like some of his nervousness was slipping away. "Because I didn't see it for the longest time—I thought I deserved the way he treated me."

"That's what abusers do. They make you dependent on them and slowly strip away your sense of self-worth so that all you have is them. You have to be a pretty strong person to break away from them." Russ looked skeptical, but Peter nodded to emphasize his point.

"How do you know so much about this?" Russ asked, but Peter heard the installers calling, and he excused himself before wheeling into the kitchen area.

"This isn't right," the lead installer said as all the men stared at the plans. "It says some piece of equipment goes in that doorway. That doesn't make sense."

"That equipment hasn't arrived yet; it should be here next week. It's a vertical grill for gyros. The opening isn't a doorway, but a place where customers can see their gyro being prepared fresh for them. The grills we ordered are polished stainless steel and meant to be seen, so the extra doorway has been converted for it," Peter explained. The installers looked skeptical and shook their heads before quietly going back to work. "Once you see it, you'll understand," he added with a smile.

"Anything you say, Petey," Rickie, the youngest of the installers teased, and the other guys laughed as well. It had taken Peter a long time to realize that when these guys picked on him like that, it meant they accepted him. Turning himself around, he went back into the other room, where he saw Russ pacing near the front windows.

"You okay?" Peter asked, and Russ swung around like he'd been slapped.

"Yes. Sorry." Russ peered out the windows again before turning back to Peter. "There are times I wish I were invisible. I keep thinking Barry's watching me, but every time I look, there's no one there. Besides, he's such a workaholic he'd never take off work at this time of the day, anyway. I know I'm being paranoid."

"That's common, from what I understand. When I was in the hospital after the car accident that damaged my legs, there was a woman in the next room whose husband beat her half to death. And once she got out, she went back to him. She said it was because of the kids and that she was afraid for them. When I asked one of the nurses, she said it happened all the time. She told me that their lives become so small that they can't figure a way out. So if you did, then you have to be pretty strong."

"Billy and Darryl helped me see what he was doing." Russ began pacing again. "It's been a week, and Barry hasn't called or tried to see me. He hasn't even stopped by the restaurant."

"Do you want him to?" Peter asked, afraid that Russ was falling into the trap.

"No," he answered vehemently. "Barry took four years of my life away, and I don't want to see him, but I keep wondering what he's planning. He loves his things, and I know now that I was just one of those possessions. He'll do something—the man's vindictive." Russ was obviously extremely concerned, and Peter wondered what he could say to help, but realized there was nothing. "I'm sorry for dumping all this on you."

Peter smiled as he glided closer to Russ. "You said there were times you wished you were invisible. I can't tell you how many times I wished I weren't." Russ turned from the window to look at him. "People seem to see the chair, not me."

"What chair?" Russ asked with a wink, making Peter smile.

Peter figured now was probably a good time to change the subject. "What sort of décor did you have in mind for the dining room?"

"The walls will be ocean blue with white trim, clean and simple. Darryl found some paintings by Greek artists that we're going to hang on the walls. We want the restaurant to feel upscale and fresh." Russ looked down at the floors covered with cardboard. "We found a really durable finish, but left the floors light so they would have the color of sand. Even in the middle of winter, the restaurant should have the look and feel of summer," Russ explained in an excited voice.

A knock on the restaurant door made Russ jump, and he walked over, peering out before opening the door. "Can I help you?" Russ asked, opening the door, and a police officer in uniform stepped inside.

"We have a report of a stolen vehicle, a white Nissan Sentra," the police officer said very officially.

"That's my car, but I didn't report it stolen," Russ answered as he began to shake.

"The report was made by a Barry Spencer."

"I can prove it. The registration is in the car." Russ walked outside, and Peter watched and waited. He heard the sounds of the installers in the kitchen, but no other sound. Shaking his head, he worried about Russ and exactly what his ex was trying to pull. After a few minutes, Russ came back inside, closing the door before leaning against it. "I guess that answers the questions about Barry the Bastard," Russ said, breathing hard.

"Is everything all right?" Richie asked as he approached Peter with the plans in hand. Without waiting for an answer, Richie showed the drawing to Peter, asked his question, and then returned to work.

"I take it the car is yours," Peter commented.

"Yes. Barry got into an accident about two years ago, and I remember now that he transferred his old car to me to save on insurance rates because his went through the roof. I guess he forgot that little fact, and it seems the police officer was not too happy about being sent on a wild goose chase," Russ said with a touch of glee before his smile faded. "I'd sort of hoped he'd give up, but that's not likely." Peter agreed, but kept his opinion to himself. Russ didn't need him adding to his worries.

"Hey. It's going to be okay," Peter said to reassure Russ. "Barry can pull whatever crap he wants, but you have friends who'll stand behind you. Remember that. You don't need Barry the Bastard anymore." Peter turned away and wheeled himself to a worktable in the corner, pulling his bag off the handles of his chair. Opening the bag, Peter pulled out his small, lightweight laptop. Russ didn't say anything, and Peter didn't hear footsteps, either. "I mean it."

"It's been a long time since I had friends," Russ murmured so softly Peter barely heard it.

"Russ," Peter began, swallowing really hard as he turned his chair to face him. "I was wondering if when we're done here, you'd like to get something to eat." Peter released the last of his breath. He fully expected to get shot down. It had happened before. Peter waited, but Russ didn't say anything, and for a while Peter wasn't sure Russ had even heard him. This was a really stupid idea, he knew that, and Peter whirled his chair around and back to the table where he'd rested his computer. No one saw him as a man, just a guy in a wheelchair. Why would Russ be any different?

"I think I'd like that," Russ said, and Peter almost missed it as he silently berated himself for asking.

Peter turned his chair so fast he felt a little dizzy. "Really?" He had to make sure he'd heard right.

"Sure." Russ smiled. "Why?"

"Nothing," Peter answered.

"I told you all the embarrassing stuff about Barry the Bastard. So now it's your turn." Peter heard Russ walk up behind him. "Why would you think I wouldn't want to have dinner with you?"

"It's really nothing." Peter sighed. "The last guy I got up the nerve to ask out to dinner looked at me like I was from outer space and told me that he didn't date cripples."

"He actually said that?"

"Word for word. The jerk," Peter spat before returning to his laptop. "A month later he even had the gall to ask for a discount on a stove he was purchasing for one of his restaurants. I told him we cripples weren't allowed to give discounts." Peter tried not to laugh at his own cleverness, and thankfully he heard Russ chuckle behind him.

"I have to be honest. I'm not sure I'm really ready to date anyone, but I'd like to go to dinner with you." Peter felt Russ's weight on the back of his chair. "And for the record, I noticed, and you are a very handsome man." Russ's breath against the back of Peter's neck had him shifting in the chair for multiple reasons, not least of which was the fact that Peter was still very much a man, and if Russ looked, that fact would be extremely visible. "When I first saw you, it wasn't the chair I noticed, but your rich olive skin and dark eyes."

Peter closed his eyes, trying not to let himself get too excited or jump ahead of things. Russ was going through a difficult breakup, and Peter could not allow himself to get his hopes up. This was just a dinner. But Russ had actually noticed him.

"I noticed you too," Peter said, feeling a bit like a high school kid, but he didn't mind a bit.

"Have you been on many dates since the accident?"

"No. I'm sort of ashamed to say that before the accident I was a bit of a slut." Peter pushed the power button on his laptop, and it began to boot up. "I went out to the bars downtown a lot. I was athletic and handsome, so I turned a lot of heads. Now heads turn, but it's often to look away. Not that I'm proud of how I was then. I was always looking for a good time. A lot of things changed after the accident, some for the better. Not that I realized it at the time."

Russ sat down in a folding chair next to him. "Like what?"

"Well, for one thing, I realized that I couldn't skate by on my looks and charm anymore. I had to knuckle down, work hard, and make something of myself. I had to be something other than the guy who could run fast and look good." Peter looked Russ in the eyes. "I also learned who my real friends were, and I didn't have many of them. Most of the guys I knew turned out to be posers who disappeared as soon as the fun ended. At the time, I thought the accident was the worst possible thing that could have happened to me. And it was pretty bad, don't get me wrong. But I think everything happens for a reason, and who knows where I'd be now if I hadn't been hurt."

"You'd probably have gone to the Olympics," Russ offered.

"Or I could be just one more athlete whose dreams were bigger than their abilities and now have a life looking back at what could have been. I guess the biggest thing I learned was to take what life gives you and make the best out of it." Peter turned back to his laptop, activating his Aircard and connecting to the office network. "It looks like the grills will ship this week, and we should have them ready to install a week later." Peter continued working his way through his e-mails. "Is it okay if I call my office?"

Russ nodded and stood up. "I need to check in with Darryl as well."

Peter got his cell phone and began returning calls, spending a good part of the morning talking with Annette, following up on orders, and setting up appointments for the next few weeks. By the time Peter hung up from his last call, Billy was walking through the front door carrying a tray.

"We figured everyone was busy working hard, so I brought food." Billy set down the tray, and Peter thought his installers had turned into a swarm of starving locusts the way they descended on the food. Peter took one of the wraps, and so did Russ, sitting back to eat while the installers finished off every other crumb.

"Don't your wives feed you?" Peter teased after swallowing a bite of cranberry chicken salad.

"Not like this," Richie said around a mouthful, and the others nodded their heads appreciatively as they continued eating.

"I'll be sure to tell Darryl you liked it," Billy said, and all the guys nodded again vigorously but didn't stop eating.

Once the food was gone, Russ and Peter gave Billy a tour of the work completed so far, and then Peter settled in to work for the afternoon, conscious the entire time of wherever Russ was. He continued working until the guys said their good-nights, and Peter gathered his things to get ready to leave.

"I'm not sure where we should go to dinner. You work at one of the best restaurants in the area, so taking you there isn't much of a treat."

"I like Thai, and there's a great place outside town. I can meet you there at six thirty if you like." Russ seemed a little nervous, and Peter hoped it was excitement as opposed to second thoughts. Russ went on to give him directions, and Peter wrote them down, quickly coming to the conclusion that Russ was truly excited about dinner.

Packing up his things, Peter left the restaurant with Russ and got himself into his car, heading home to change for his first date in a long time, his excitement threatening to spill out of him and fill the car. Peter had found Russ attractive almost since he first saw him, and he'd given up on ever having this kind of opportunity again.

At the house, Peter got himself inside and into his bedroom, changing into fresh clothes and leaving again, following Russ's directions to the restaurant and pulling into the parking lot a minute or two early. One of the hardest things Peter had had to learn after the accident was that he didn't get anywhere in a hurry anymore. Everything took longer, even something as simple as getting in and out of the car.

Rolling across the parking lot, Peter panicked when he suddenly found he didn't have control of his chair anymore. "It's just me," Russ said happily. "I saw you getting out of your car." Peter put his hands on his lap and let Russ guide him into the restaurant. "It's really tight between the tables," Russ said as he looked around. "I never realized that before. When you come back, would you check the plans for the restaurant to make sure there's enough room for a wheelchair to move comfortably between the tables? The law says thirty inches, but that's probably not enough." Peter felt Russ's hand on his shoulder and instantly wanted more of that touch, but he reminded himself it was probably a simple gesture and nothing more.

"A table for two please," Peter said when he saw the hostess approach, and she led them around the tables, with Peter barely able to get through. She did take away one of the chairs, though, and Peter settled himself at the table, taking the offered menu. "What do you like?" he asked, once Russ had settled in his seat.

"The pineapple fried rice with chicken. It's a large portion, so we could get that and something else to share."

"Sounds good," Peter said. "You choose, because after all, you're the chef." Peter winked, as Russ studied his menu, and when the server came over, they ordered their drinks and Russ ordered the food—fried rice and pad Thai. How had he known what Peter liked? Amazing. "Do you have family?" Peter asked, taking a sip of his water.

"Not anymore. My parents are gone, and I was an only child. Mom and Dad didn't think they could ever have kids, and as she got older, Mom thought she was going through the change of life. Instead, she had me. Dad was older than Mom, so by the time I graduated high school he'd already been retired for a while, and Mom turned sixty-five that same year. She died of cancer a couple years ago, and Dad died within a few months. I was working by then, and six months later, I met Barry. They would have hated him on sight. I guess that should have been my first clue." Russ gulped his water, and the server brought their drinks before refilling the water glasses. "Do you have a big family?"

"Not anymore. I had a sister, Diane, but she died when we were kids. She got sick, and by the time Mom and Dad got her to the hospital it was too late. I don't know what she had. Mom and Dad never talked about it. My mom's gone too, so now I just have my dad. He's pretty spry and a lot of fun." Peter smiled when he thought of his dad. "I visit him almost every weekend. Lately he's decided to sell the house and move into a retirement home. It'll be easier on him, now that he doesn't have to take care of Mama's house, as he calls it. I lived with them after the accident, but it was hard on Mama, so I worked hard to become independent, and once I got a good job, bought my own small house." Russ had rested his hand on the table, and Peter touched Russ's fingers, feeling them slide into his. The warmth of Russ's skin felt incredible against Peter's hand, and he lightly ran his finger over Russ's work-roughened skin, wondering what his hand would feel like touching other parts of his body.

For a second, Peter waited for Russ to say something, but he stared over Peter's shoulder, pulling his hand away from Peter's. His eyes got wider and his mouth hung open. "What is it?" Peter asked before turning in his chair in time to see Barry striding toward their table. Turning back, he saw that Russ had gone pale and appeared to be shaking slightly. "It's okay. He can't do anything here."

"W… what are you doing here?" Russ sounded so small, and he looked like he was trying to sink into his chair.

"I came to get you," Barry said softly but with more than a hint of determination. "It's been a week, and now it's time to come home." Barry grabbed one of Russ's wrists, and Peter could see Barry's grip tightening.

"You're hurting me," Russ whispered and tried to pull his arm away. Peter could see the pain and embarrassment in Russ's eyes.

"Stop it. He doesn't want to go anywhere with you." Peter felt completely helpless. He couldn't stand up to Barry and he couldn't stop him from hurting Russ. All he could do was watch.

"What, you're dating cripples now? How pathetic." Barry lifted Russ out of his seat.

"Leave him alone," Peter said. Spending these last few years in a chair, he'd gotten used to the change in view. Rarely was he at eye level, and never had he thought that a particular advantage, until today. When Barry moved close enough, Peter jabbed him with his elbow as hard as he could. Barry let go of Russ's arm, clutching himself in the middle of the restaurant. Other people turned their way, hearing his cry over the noise from the other diners. Thankfully, Barry had had enough and made his way to the exit, walking funny the entire way. "Are you okay? Do you want me to call some help?"

Russ rubbed his wrist and looked miserable. "No, I'm fine."

Russ didn't sound okay. "He's done that before." Peter had seen the bruises.

"Yes. Since I'm smaller than him, he liked to treat me like I'm some sort of child," Russ answered, still massaging his skin.

"We could get our food to go if you want," Peter offered, and Russ nodded. Peter flagged down their waiter and explained the situation. A few minutes later, after paying the bill, they left the restaurant, with Russ carrying their food in Styrofoam containers. "My house isn't too far from here. We could go there," Peter offered.

Russ agreed without saying anything, and Peter got into his car. Driving slowly so Russ could follow, he took the easiest route to his house.

In his garage, Peter got out of his car. Normally he'd put the door down, but he left it open today so he could wait for Russ. Peter had shifted into his chair and was wheeling himself inside before Russ joined him. Peter wondered why Russ had sat in his car for so long, but he refrained from asking. What happened with Barry had to have upset him, and if Russ needed a few minutes alone, that was his prerogative.

Russ followed him inside but didn't say anything. He just stood in the doorway holding the bag of food. "Go on and have a seat. I'll get the plates and stuff," Peter said, and he moved though the kitchen as fast as he dared before returning and setting the plates and silverware on the table. Russ hadn't moved.

"Maybe I should go," Russ said before placing the bag on the table. Peter didn't want that. He very much wanted Russ to stay, and he hated the thought of Barry ruining the evening. Reaching out, he caught Russ by the wrist. At first he saw Russ glare at him, a spark of fear flashing in Russ's eyes like when he'd seen Barry, and Peter nearly let go. But instead, he lightly caressed Russ's skin.

"All of us are not like Barry," Peter said, holding Russ's hand, loving the feel of his skin as Peter ran his thumb along the back. "We don't hit or hurt, and we don't need to control everything and everyone."

"But the things he said to you," Russ mumbled.

"If you want my opinion, Barry will say whatever he thinks will get him the control he desperately needs. I bet you've heard him say the meanest things before turning around and being the sweetest man you've ever known." Russ nodded slowly. "That's all part of being in control. I know, because after the accident I acted that way for a while."

"You did?" Russ asked, and he slowly moved toward the table, but to Peter's gratitude, he didn't let go of his hand. "I find that hard to believe." Slowly Russ lowered himself into a chair, but made no move toward the food.

Peter reached for the bag and managed to snag it with his fingers. Getting out the food, he placed some of each dish on both their plates before putting Russ's in the microwave for thirty seconds. Peter's kitchen was a model of efficiency, though it had taken him a long time to get everything just where he needed it. "I was awful," Peter said, taking out Russ's plate, replacing it with his own. "I couldn't walk, and everything in my life felt out of control. I was at the mercy and patience of everyone around me. I yelled and screamed at people, called my mom every awful thing I could think of, and would then apologize if the yelling didn't work." The microwave dinged and Peter pulled out his plate. "It wasn't until I stopped being so angry that I got what I wanted. I started making progress and learned how to master the wheelchair."

Russ shook his head. "I can't see that at all. You're nothing like Barry." Finally, Russ lifted his fork and took a tentative bite of his food.

"Not now, but I was then, sort of, I guess. Lying in a hospital bed, I couldn't control anything about my life. People I didn't know were even trying to make decisions about what I would eat. I'd get poked and prodded when they said. Hell, I couldn't even go to the bathroom on my own. So I did whatever I thought would get me what I wanted."

"But you never hurt anyone?"

"Physically, no. But I was a complete shit to just about everyone, especially those trying to help me." Peter ate a bite of the rice. "Would you like something to drink? I have beer and soda."

"A Coke would be great," Russ answered, and Peter glided to the refrigerator, got two cans, and handed one to Russ. "What happens when Barry comes back? He could hurt you."

Peter shook his head. "I'm not afraid of him, but I am worried about you. He was obviously following you and may have been for a while, because he wouldn't have known where you were otherwise. I don't think him being at the restaurant was an accident."

"It wasn't," Russ agreed. "Barry never does anything by accident. Everything is deliberate and thought out. He thought he could intimidate me into coming with him." Russ looked down at his plate. "I'm ashamed to say if you weren't there, it probably would have worked." Russ took another few bites before setting down his fork. "I'd hoped he would just write me off and find someone else. I should have known it wouldn't be so easy. He never loved me, I know that now, no matter what he told me. I was just another piece of property to him, a possession."

"Someone he could control."

"Yes." Russ picked up his fork again, and they ate, with only the sound of their forks on the plates to break the quiet. "I can't believe I was so pathetic to think Barry loved me."

"You aren't pathetic, and everyone deserves and wants to be loved. There's nothing wrong with that." Peter sipped from his soda can before picking up his fork again. "You can see what Barry was doing now, and I think that's the difference."

"I guess," Russ said with a shrug.

Peter ate quietly, looking over at Russ between bites. "Do you want to go back to Barry?" He knew it sounded like a strange question, but he had to ask it.

"No," Russ said, and the answer seemed to surprise him. Then he smiled. "I really don't."

"Then Barry can't make you. He can follow you around, but it's just a waste of his time. He can try to intimidate you, but he's the one who'll end up in trouble because he can't make you do what you don't want to." Peter couldn't stop a smile when he finally saw a glimpse of the excitement from Russ that had been present before Barry had made his ill-timed and unwelcome appearance. The rest of the meal seemed much lighter without Barry casting such a heavy shadow over Russ. When they were done, Russ helped him carry the dishes to the sink.

"Do you need me to help clean up?"

"No. I can load the dishwasher," Peter said as he turned away from the sink.

"Thank you for a nice dinner and for your support," Russ told him in a gentle voice. "I know we haven't known each other very long, but it means a lot." Russ took Peter's hand and leaned forward. At first Peter wasn't sure what was happening, and then his brain kicked in and he nearly gasped as Russ kissed him. Peter closed his eyes, returning the kiss, his head tingling a little. He wanted to put his arms around Russ's neck and draw him in closer so he could show Russ just how much he wanted him. Peter wanted Russ so badly, but he resisted the urge to do what his body was demanding so forcefully. Russ wasn't ready for that, and somewhere in the back of his mind, Peter thought he'd better let Russ set the pace or he'd run the risk of scaring him off.

Peter kept his eyes closed as the kiss softened, and then Russ's lips pulled away. Peter waited a few seconds before opening his eyes again to see Russ staring back at him. "I really should be going," Russ said, and Peter nodded.

"I'll see you Monday, and we should be able to finish installing the equipment." Peter hoped he'd be seeing Russ before then, but he wasn't going to push.

"Good night," Russ said before leaving through the back door. Peter watched and smiled as he left, the door closing behind him. Peter finished cleaning up the kitchen before getting ready for bed. He tried watching television and reading to calm his mind, but whenever he closed his eyes, he could feel that kiss. And once he climbed into bed, the words "Russ kissed me" played in his head again and again. Peter knew it was almost sophomoric and that he was probably setting himself up for a letdown, but Russ had kissed him.

CHAPTER FOUR

RUSS unlocked the front door to Billy and Darryl's house, walking inside before quickly closing the door behind him. Leaving Peter's, he'd been happy. He could hardly believe he'd kissed Peter. Not that he was disappointed, and from the look on Peter's face, he hadn't been, either. He still wondered what had possessed him to do that, but it had definitely been nice. What was bothering Russ was how badly he wanted to kiss Peter again. He'd just gotten away from Barry and was beginning to get over him. Peter was a sweet, caring man, and Russ didn't want him to be some rebound guy. Peter deserved better than that.

Footsteps outside the front door made Russ tense. Once he'd parked the car, Russ had thought he heard footsteps behind him. He hadn't been sure, so he'd hurried to the door and gone right inside. The footsteps stopped, and Russ peered out through the peephole to see Barry staring back at him. The door was locked, and Russ had no intention of opening it. The knocker banged, and Russ jumped slightly, but stayed where he was and didn't move. The knock sounded again. "I know you're there, Russ. I saw you go inside." There were windows on either side of the door, so Russ hugged the back of it and remained out of sight, his heart pounding in his ears. "I just want to talk to you. Please open the door." Barry's voice was softer, and Russ knew that tone. Yelling hadn't worked, so Barry filled his voice with honey.

"Go home, Barry. I have nothing to say to you." Russ rested with his back against the door, too scared to move.

Russ felt Barry pound on the door, the vibrations shooting through his body. "We need to talk."

"No. You need to leave or I'll call the police," Russ said with as much force as he could muster. "You aren't welcome here."

"I just want to talk." Barry's voice sounded calm, but after talking with Peter, Russ now had an idea he was just being played. He'd always fallen for it before, but he wasn't going to this time.

"I don't. So go home," Russ said as he fished his cell phone out of his pocket, waving it in front of the window. "I was serious about calling the police. Now leave." He could hardly believe how good it felt to say that to Barry. In his own way, he was standing up to him. Maybe not face to face, but he was doing it nonetheless. Barry went quiet, and Russ listened for footsteps, but he didn't hear those, either. He couldn't see anything in the peephole, but he didn't think Barry was ready to give up yet. Moving away from the door, he hurried to the front windows, and when he peered out, he saw nothing but an empty front step.

A soft, high-pitched sound reached Russ's ears, and he realized it was the gate by the side of the house squeaking. Russ rushed through the house and up the stairs, tripping and falling onto his hands, but he kept going anyway. He locked himself in the bathroom as he fumbled with his phone, dropping it on the floor in his rush before scooping it up again.

"Russ," he heard Billy call from the back of the house. "Are you here?"

"Upstairs," he answered, opening the bathroom door, and he heard Billy rushing up the stairs. "I saw Barry walking away from the house. Are you okay?"

"Yes. I didn't let him in, and when I heard the gate, I thought he was going around to the back." Russ's heart was pounding again, and he tried to catch his breath. "But that was you?" Russ's fear began to abate.

"Yeah. I didn't mean to frighten you. The boys are out back in the yard. Charles and Marie are going to pick them up in the morning, so I was about to make them a snack. You can join us if you want," Billy offered.

"What if Barry comes back and hurts the boys? I shouldn't stay here." Russ could feel the panic rising inside him again.

"Barry isn't going to hurt anyone anymore. In the morning, we'll call Robert and see if he has any advice."

"You're going to call the judge?"

"No. I'm going to call Sebastian's husband, Robert. The fact that he's a judge is a bonus." Billy winked and smiled at him. "The only person who needs to worry about Barry showing up here is Barry, because I'll rip his nuts off if he tries to hurt you or my brothers."

Russ looked into Billy's eyes and began to laugh. "Okay." Barry seemed to have a target painted on his nuts today.

"What's so funny?"

"You'll have to get in line," Russ said, and then he told Billy what Peter had done to Barry at dinner. "He walked out of the restaurant hunched over, hands grasping at his balls. Peter has great aim." Billy began to laugh, and Russ felt himself letting go of most of the alarm he'd felt.

"I've got a bottle of wine ready to go. Let's go out back. It's a great night, and we can talk." Billy walked down the stairs with him, and Russ followed Billy through the house and out into the small, but fenced backyard. The space was largely paved, with raised beds around the sides and up along the house. "Have a seat. I'll be right back," Billy said. Russ watched the boys play, building things with a huge pile of Legos they'd dumped on the patio. They appeared to be building a huge tower, and as he watched, he noticed how little they talked to one another as they worked, like they already knew what the other would do.

Billy returned carrying a tray with glasses, wine, snacks, and two juice boxes. The boys came over, and each took a juice box and the container of cashews over to where they were working. "So how was dinner with Peter?"

Russ watched the boys. "Nice. But after Barry showed up we got our order to go and went to Peter's place to eat. He's a really nice guy, not at all what I expected." Billy raised his eyebrows but didn't say anything. "I was expecting a bookish guy who hadn't done much because he was in a wheelchair. I found out that Peter's pretty cool. Before his accident he was a track star. He's also training to race wheelchairs." Billy poured them each a glass of wine and handed one to Russ. "He told me before the accident he was sort of a party animal."

"That's not a surprise," Billy said, sipping his wine, and Russ shrugged as he looked to where the boys were finishing up their tower.

"He kissed me," Russ said softly. "Or I guess I kissed him, but then he kissed me, and...." Russ stopped his babbling, wondering what Billy's reaction would be. "It was nice." Russ took another drink of wine, peering over at Billy, who seemed to be smiling into his glass.

Davey walked over to where they were talking, standing next to Billy and whispering in his ear. "Who is it?" he heard Billy whisper, and Davey said something else. Billy said something back to him, and Davey motioned to Donnie, both boys going in the house. "You deserve to be happy, and you weren't with Barry," Billy said while motioning toward the fence.

"I know. It wasn't all bad, but the last year or so, things weren't very good," Russ said before taking another gulp of his wine, wondering just what was going on. Donnie and Davey came out of the house, each carrying a huge water gun, and Davey carried a bucket as well that he handed to Billy, who put his finger in front of his lips. The boys walked to the back fence gate, and Billy motioned to them to wait as he climbed onto the edge of the flowerbed, where he could just see over the fence. Russ watched as Billy nodded, and the boys threw open the gate and began firing. Someone yelped, and Billy threw the bucket of water, which was followed by a high-pitched cry. "Eavesdropping is a bad habit, Barry," Billy called as the boys stepped back into the yard and closed the gate. "Go home and stay away."

"I just wanted to talk to him," Russ heard over the fence, Barry's teeth chattering from the cold water.

"If he wants to talk to you, he'll call. Don't make us get a restraining order!" Billy yelled over the fence, and a few moments later Russ saw him flip Barry the bird. "Next time the guns will be loaded with red wine." Billy stepped down, and the boys high-fived him and each other before putting the guns down. The back gate opened, and Russ tensed until he saw Darryl come through. The boys rushed to give him hugs and to tell Darryl all about their military maneuvers. They even had Russ smiling by the time they were done.

"Okay," Darryl said as he sank into a chair. "Finish your snack and clean up the toys. It's almost time for bed." The boys didn't argue, each taking a chair. They finished eating and worked together to clean up the Legos before hugging Billy and Darryl good night. The surprise came for Russ when they hugged him, too, and then walked inside.

"I'll be up to tuck you in," Billy called behind them, and a few minutes later he got up and followed the boys inside. Russ and Darryl talked as Russ finished his wine, and then he, too, said good night and went inside. He met Billy on the way and said good night to him as well before climbing the stairs to the small back bedroom he was using. After cleaning up and getting undressed, he climbed into bed behind a closed door. Russ had no idea why the tears came now or why exactly he was crying, but he let them come.

THE following day was Saturday, and they were always busy at Café Belgie on the weekend. Russ worked in the kitchen, with Darryl acting as his sous chef. "You need to get used to being in charge of the kitchen," Darryl had told him, and while Russ was nervous, once he'd settled into his groove, things ran smoothly and they worked great together. Darryl had promised him that when they opened the new restaurant, it would be the two of them in the kitchen to start, just like now, with Darryl to support him. The order printer that had been going solid for hours was finally slowing down, and Russ filled the last orders before starting the cleanup process.

The kitchen door opened, and Sebastian stepped in across from where Russ was working. "Barry is out front, and he wants to talk to you," Sebastian told him sympathetically.

"I don't want to see him," Russ said, and he was about to ask Sebastian to tell him to leave, but that wasn't Sebastian's responsibility, it was his. Wiping his hands, Russ walked around the prep station and entered the dining room. Barry stood near the door, looking impatient, and Russ nearly laughed when he saw Peter roll into the restaurant just then. He knew the instant Peter saw Barry because of the glare on his face. Making up his mind to do this, Russ walked over to where Barry stood. "What do you want? I'm working."

"We need to talk," Barry said firmly.

"There's nothing to talk about. It's over, I've left and I'm not coming back," Russ said with more confidence than he felt. Barry flinched, and Russ saw Peter glide next to him. Peter didn't say anything, but for a second Russ thought he saw Barry move to cover himself.

"You need to leave," another voice added from behind him, and Russ turned around to see Sebastian's husband, Robert, join the group. "I believe that Russ has told you repeatedly that he'll call you when he's ready to talk, and you need to respect that."

"And you are…?" Barry pressed.

"Judge Fortier," Robert supplied firmly, and Russ saw Barry flinch. "As I said, he'll call you. Do not follow him or show up where he lives, or where he works." Russ hadn't talked to Robert, but Billy certainly seemed to have filled him in. Barry stared wide-eyed at

Robert before he walked toward the door without saying a word. He looked back and actually opened his mouth but closed it again, the door swinging closed behind him.

The door opened again and an older, slightly disheveled man walked in. "Sweeper," Billy said with a smile as he hurried across the dining room. "Do you need some coffee, or would you like something cooler?" Billy asked as he led the man to a table and out of earshot.

"What's with him?" Peter asked as he followed Billy and Sweeper with his eyes.

"It's quite a story," Russ answered. "I only got parts of it from Billy, but he's a former homeless man that Billy befriended years ago, and it seems almost everyone here has sort of adopted him. The judge helped him get the government benefits he's been entitled to, so now he has a place to live. Billy insists he stop in every day for something to drink." Russ shifted his gaze to Peter. "Did you come in for lunch?"

"No. Actually, I came in to see how late you were working." Peter looked excited and nervous at the same time.

"I came in early this morning, so I'm done in about an hour. Why?"

Peter fidgeted in his chair, and Russ could tell he was a little nervous. "You don't have to or anything, but I usually go see my dad and take him out to dinner most Saturdays, and I stopped to see if you'd like to go with me." Peter actually rubbed the back of his neck, which was incredibly endearing. Even when he and Barry had first met, Barry hadn't exactly asked Russ—he'd simply suggested forcefully, and Russ had rearranged his schedule. Peter's way was really nice.

"Are you sure you want me to horn in on your time with your dad?"

Peter shook his head. "You and my dad will get along great. He loves to cook, and he'll talk your ear off."

"You're serious—you want me to meet your dad?" Russ felt a touch of glee and trepidation at the same time. Peter was asking him to meet his father. He hadn't met Peter all that long ago, and he wasn't sure if he was ready for a "meet the parents" thing.

Peter lightly touched his hand. "Yeah, Dad loves to meet new people, and he doesn't get out as much as he used to."

"Okay. I can be ready in little over an hour. So if you're willing to wait, I'll ride out to your dad's with you." Russ thought maybe meeting Peter's dad could be really cool, and it would be nice. He tried not to think about the possible implications too much.

"Cool. I have an errand I need to run, but I'll be back then." Peter released his hand and glided toward the door, and Russ thought he saw him smiling the entire time. As soon as the restaurant door closed behind Peter, the ribbing began, and Russ hurried back to the kitchen to get away from Billy and Sebastian, who had a habit of playing off each other.

In the kitchen, Russ saw Darryl giving him looks, and he went back to work, ignoring everyone until Darryl started laughing. "Have fun, don't worry," Darryl said, raising his voice when Billy came into the kitchen, "and don't listen to my queeny partner." Billy humphed and promptly left the kitchen again. Russ began to laugh, and Darryl joined him.

"You're going to pay for that remark you know," Russ commented. Darryl nodded, but he didn't look too worried. Billy and Darryl were the strongest, happiest couple Russ knew, and he very much wanted what they had. He'd thought he might someday have been able to have that with Barry, but he realized now that was impossible.

Russ got to work, filling the last few orders that came straggling in and helping with the changeover to dinner service. Once Russ was done, Darryl shooed him out of the kitchen, and he changed his clothes before entering the dining room, where Peter sat at one of the tables with a coffee cup, waiting for him. "Are you ready?" Peter looked up and smiled. "I hope you weren't waiting too long."

"Nope," Peter answered, and he looked around. Billy told him he'd get the cup, and after waving goodbye, they left the restaurant, and Russ followed Peter to his car. Peter got behind the wheel, and Russ wondered if there was something he could do to help, but Peter seemed to take care of everything and quickly had his chair stowed, so Russ got into the passenger seat, and Peter pulled out of his parking space. Russ found he was interested in the hand controls built into Peter's car. He could accelerate and brake using a handle mounted just below the steering wheel. It was fascinating for Russ to watch.

"Did you have to relearn how to drive?" Russ asked as they rode down the highway. Peter had explained that his dad lived in Hershey, so they had nearly an hour ride ahead of them.

"Sort of, but it wasn't difficult. Once the car was converted, it just took some time for me to get used to the new controls. The hard part was getting myself to stop thinking I could use my feet," Peter said. "There are still times when I forget and think I can do something that I can't. Parts of my brain still think my legs can move. It gets less frequent, but it still happens."

"You seem so... comfortable with who you are," Russ commented. "There are times when I have no idea who I am."

"I didn't have a choice, and you'll feel better after some time. Barry made himself the center of your life and now that's gone. But you'll heal and move on," Peter told him, and Russ nodded, turning to look out the window.

They continued making small talk, and Russ got more and more nervous the closer they got to Peter's dad's. He wasn't so sure this was a good idea, but he'd agreed to come, and it was too late now to back out. Peter exited the highway, heading toward town. "Are you sure this is okay?" Russ asked nervously, his stomach churning.

"Of course," Peter answered lightly before making another turn and parking in front of a small house. Russ looked at the house and wondered how Peter could have lived in the small two-story home. It didn't seem conducive for him. "After the accident, Mom and Dad made a room for me in the back on the first floor," Peter explained, like he was reading Russ's mind.

Peter opened the car door, and Russ got the chair out from behind him. Once he'd transferred himself to the chair, Peter rolled up the walk. The front door opened, and an older man walked out slowly to meet them. "Dad, this is Russ," Peter said, introducing him once he'd been hugged. "Russ, this is my dad, Costa."

"It's nice to meet you, sir," Russ said as they shook hands.

"Welcome, young man. It's always nice to meet Peter's friends," he said, motioning toward the house. "He didn't tell me he was bringing anyone."

Russ looked at Peter, a little concerned.

"Dad," Peter started. "Russ is the man I told you about. He's a chef, and in a few weeks he's going to be running his own restaurant, a Greek restaurant. I was hoping you could share some of Mom's recipes with him."

Russ could feel Costa looking him over. "He doesn't look Greek."

"I'm not, sir. But I've learned a lot about Greek cooking." The sound Peter's father made gave Russ pause, and he looked at Peter for help, wondering if it was safe for him to go inside. Even Peter seemed startled.

"You do not learn Greek cooking from a book." He turned around to Russ. "You come inside, and I show you how to cook Greek. Peter usually takes me out for dinner, but tonight we cook." Costa led them into the house, and they ended up in the kitchen, where Costa opened the refrigerator and began pulling out ingredients. "The secret to Greek food is in the spices."

"What are you making, Dad?"

"I'm showing him how to make your mother's spanakopita," Costa explained, and he continued setting things on the counter. He also set a bottle of wine on the counter before opening it and getting three glasses. "Cooking without wine is like sex alone. You may get the job done, but you don't really care once it's over."

"Dad!" Peter cried as he rolled his eyes.

Russ laughed and some of his nervousness slipped away. "I agree with you." Russ lifted his glass to Costa before taking a drink. The wine was awful, but Russ said nothing. Costa took a drink as well. His eyes went wide, and he spit his mouthful into the sink. "Boy, you should have said something. Peter, wash the glasses and pour that into the sink. I'll get another bottle." Russ poured out his glass and listened as Costa went into the basement. A few minutes later he returned with a box, a bottle of wine sitting in the top. "The neighbor gave me that, and I should have known," he said referring to the awful wine. Costa set the box on the counter before handing Russ the wine. "Open this. It should be much better."

Russ picked up the corkscrew from the counter and began opening the wine.

"What's in the box, Dad?"

"Some things I thought you should have. There are three more boxes in the basement. You can take them home with you." Costa poured the wine once Russ got the dry cork out, and said he wasn't holding out much hope that this bottle would be any better than the last one, but it definitely was. Once the wine situation seemed to be remedied, Costa got down to work explaining to him how to make the dough. "Are these on your menu?" he asked, referring to the spanakopita.

"Yes, along with various types of souvlaki, as well as moussaka. And we'll be serving gyros."

"We have real gyros grills on order," Peter explained.

Costa made that sound again. "At the church festival last year, they made gyros using frozen patties." It was obvious what Costa thought of the frozen patties.

"I'm getting the real meat shipped in as well," Russ explained as he worked with the phyllo dough Costa had gotten out of the refrigerator. He hadn't expected to be cooking this evening, but he was having a good time.

"Now, the secret to the filling is the right amount of cheese and spinach," Costa explained and demonstrated the technique for Russ, and Russ nodded, repeating the technique multiple times. As he worked, Russ found himself looking over at Peter all the time, smiling, and seeing the other man's sweet smile in return. More than once Russ moved closer to the counter so no one could see what he knew had to be a pronounced bulge in his pants. Peter was hot, and when he smiled, he went from smoldering to incredibly gorgeous, especially when his eyes sparkled like they did right now. Costa kept telling Russ about the food, and all he could see were the tiny dimples on Peter's face.

"Dad." Peter rolled closer. "I think we have enough for an army." He was laughing, and Russ looked down at the counter covered in small pastry triangles and began to laugh too.

"I guess I lost track of what I was doing," Russ said, letting go of the worry and concern that had been a part of his life for so long now. He hadn't thought of Barry or anything other than Peter and working with his hands the entire time, and it felt amazing.

Russ saw Costa look at him and then Peter, and back to him again as if he were trying to figure something out, but he said nothing, to Russ's relief. He liked Peter, that was becoming obvious to him, and he'd loved Peter's kiss, but he wasn't sure if he should get into any relationship right now. Russ blinked at the thought and silently laughed at himself. They'd kissed, and he liked being with Peter, but everything was so muddled.

He jumped and turned when he felt a touch on his cheek. Peter was wiping him gently with a cloth. "You have flour on your cheek," Peter said as he lowered his hand, the smile slipping from his face. "Sorry."

Peter turned away, and Russ looked around the room, seeing Costa glaring at them, and Russ knew where Peter's happiness had gone. He didn't know what to do, but it seemed that Peter's father had a problem with him being gay, or at least with bringing home a…

what, boyfriend? Russ pushed the thought out of his mind, moving closer to Peter. "It's okay. I understand," he said softly before returning to where Costa appeared to be waiting for him. He felt self-conscious and a lot of the fun was now gone as Costa and Peter stared across the kitchen at each other. Then, without a word, Peter wheeled himself out of the room, casting a killing look at his father, who threw his towel on the counter before looking at him.

Russ turned away and thought about following Peter, but Costa beat him to it, and Russ found himself alone in the kitchen. Thankfully, Costa had set out baking sheets, and Russ began transferring the small triangles from the work area.

"How could you do that?" Costa's voice drifted in from the other room, filled with hurt.

"Do what, Dad? Bring someone to meet you who I might like and who may like me? What's bothering you? I told you I was gay a long time ago. This should not be a shock." Peter sounded hurt, and Russ had the urge to go to him. But that wasn't his place. "What did you think, that I would outgrow being gay, or that the accident would change that?"

"I guess I hoped…," Costa began, and the rest of the words faded away as his voice got softer. Russ closed his eyes, hoping that meant they were talking instead of yelling. "You never bring anyone home, and I thought…." More fragments reached Russ's ears, and he tried his best not to listen, moving around the kitchen and away from the door.

"Dad, I—" He heard Peter's voice as he put the last of the spanakopita on the sheets. "He actually sees me, and I like him." Russ thought he might have heard Peter's voice break, and then nothing at all. Russ tried to keep his mind on what he was doing and away from what might be happening in the other room. At least he wasn't hearing angry voices anymore, and he took comfort in that. Deciding to play dumb, he set aside the last pan before walking from the kitchen into the living room.

"Costa, how long…." Russ turned the corner to the living room and saw Peter still sitting in his chair, with Costa hugging his son. Neither one made a sound, and Russ backed up as quietly as he could before retreating to the kitchen, where he waited until he heard what sounded like normal voices again. After a few minutes, he heard footsteps, and Costa strode into the kitchen, turning on the oven. Peter followed, and he looked both happy and sad at the same time, but it appeared to Russ that the happiness might be starting to win.

"We need to bake for twenty minutes," Costa said while they waited for the oven to finish heating. Russ looked at the other two, trying to get some idea if they were okay now or not.

"Do you like my son?" Costa asked as he turned away from the oven, his expression serious. Russ didn't know what to say. They'd just met, and he was still trying to figure himself out.

"Dad," Peter said, "you don't get to ask that."

"Well, I want to know if he is going to hurt you." Costa looked at both of them.

Russ wasn't sure how to answer and decided to be as truthful as possible. "Not on purpose," he said softly, feeling uncomfortable and a bit put out.

"Dad, that's enough," Peter said, and Costa seemed to understand. Opening the oven door, Costa placed the sheets inside and set the timer. "I know you mean well, but…."

"It's okay, Peter. Your dad doesn't want you to get hurt, and I understand that," Russ said, feeling a bit strange in what had become a slightly surreal setting. He did understand, and if his parents had been alive, Russ would hope they would show the same concern for him that Costa was demonstrating for Peter. Walking to where Peter sat, Russ took his hand and squeezed it before letting it go. Russ found a seat at the table and waited. He wasn't sure what he was waiting for, but he felt out of place and like he was imposing on what should be a private discussion between Peter and his father.

Costa turned away and began to make what looked like a salad while Peter reached to the counter and pulled the box his father had brought up from the basement into his lap. Wheeling over to the table, Peter moved into the empty space next to him and opened the top. Russ resisted the urge to look inside.

The timer went off, and Peter closed the box. "Would you like me to set that somewhere for you?" Russ asked, getting ready to take the box from Peter.

"Set it by the front door, and I'll add the others to it," Costa told him, and Russ complied. When he returned, Peter and Costa were talking quietly. He noticed the spanakopita cooling on the counter.

Russ turned and left the kitchen, sitting in the living room, where he picked up a magazine off the coffee table and waited quietly. They needed to talk, and they didn't need him to listen in. After a while, Russ felt his eyes drifting closed, and he jerked himself awake when Peter said his name. "I'm sorry, Russ. Maybe this wasn't the best idea."

"It's okay, Peter. You and your dad have things you need to talk about, and bringing me here seems to have brought things into the open." Russ sighed through a stifled yawn. "Sorry."

"Dinner's ready. Come in and eat, and I'll take you home," Peter promised with a half smile, and Russ got up and followed him into the kitchen. The table had been set, and Russ took the place Costa indicated.

"Thank you for coming, Russ," Costa said, "and for being so polite." He raised his wine glass and smiled. "Peter and I have not talked in a long while, but we did today, so thank you."

Russ had no idea why Costa was thanking him, but he smiled and raised his glass, noticing that Peter did as well. The food was amazing, and Russ agreed that the mixture Costa had shown him for the spanakopita was perfect, with the right flavors and textures. Not that he'd had much doubt, and he reminded himself to try to get Peter's mother's recipe for moussaka before he left.

The dinner itself was quiet, with a lot of eating and not much talking, which was fine. Once they were stuffed, they drank another glass of wine, making small talk.

After cleaning up the dishes, Peter said goodbye to his father. Costa asked Russ to help with the boxes he had for Peter, and Russ gladly helped load them in Peter's trunk. After another round of goodbyes, Peter and Russ left the house, with Russ carrying a bag of food.

"I'm sorry about this," Peter said after they'd driven about halfway back to Peter's house. "I told both my mom and dad I was gay a long time ago, and I thought he was okay with it."

Russ shifted in the seat. "For starters, you can stop apologizing. Your dad was pretty cool, and it's obvious that he loves you a lot. Sometimes I really miss that. Maybe that's why I ended up with Barry the Bastard. I jumped at the first guy I thought might love me. But your dad really does, and there are much worse things than that. He's only concerned because he cares." Russ looked out the side window. "Did you and your dad have a good talk?"

"I think so, yeah. My dad said he liked you," Peter told him. "He said you were honest, and he told me to bring you back so you can cook together again."

"If I remember right, you told me that you hadn't been out with anyone since the accident."

"No," Peter answered.

"Did you ever introduce anyone to your folks before the accident?"

"No. I always thought they didn't want to know about that part of my life. I was gay and I'd told them, but...." Peter slowed down as they came up to a bottleneck on the highway. "There was never anyone I wanted to introduce them to." Traffic slowed to a stop, and Peter looked over at him.

"Why me?" Russ asked softly.

"Because I like you," Peter answered, and then traffic started to move slowly. "Because... I don't know. I guess because I wanted to give you or show you something I hadn't with anyone else ever." Peter stopped just behind the car in front of him. "No one looks at me twice, and you did, I think." Peter huffed. "I know I'm being stupid for thinking you could like me or want to be with me or anything, but I guess I asked you because I wanted you to meet my dad." Russ smiled, and Peter scowled at him. "Are you making fun of me?"

"No. I'm smiling because I like you too. I don't know if it's too soon, and it probably is, so I don't know… and it looks like it's my turn to ramble. But I do, and I meant what I said to your dad. I can't make any promises, but I won't hurt you on purpose." Traffic began to move ahead of them again, and Peter sped up. After a few seconds, Russ started laughing and couldn't stop.

"What's so funny?"

"That was the most high school conversation I've had since high school." Russ leaned forward and rested his head on the dash. "How about we make a deal," Russ continued, once he could breathe. "Once we get to your house we can talk."

Traffic thinned out ahead of them, and Peter got back up to speed. "Okay, we'll talk." Russ could hear the trepidation in Peter's voice and wondered where that came from.

Finally arriving home, Peter pulled into his garage and closed the door. "Would you help me with the boxes from my dad?" he asked without getting out of the car. "I'm sorry about all of this."

Russ nodded and turned to get out of the car, but then stopped, swiveling to face Peter. He wanted to tell Peter that he was a nice man, attractive and funny, but he knew the words wouldn't be believed any more than he would believe them if they were said to him. So instead he leaned over the seat, touching Peter's cheek with his hand, and kissed him. Not some chaste peck or a light brush, but he really kissed him, hard, full, and demanding. "Did anyone ever tell you that sometimes you talk too much?" Russ asked, and Peter nodded briefly before Russ kissed him again, this time tugging him closer, fingers threading through Peter's soft hair.

Moving away only once he needed to get his breath, Russ stared at Peter with wide eyes. He wasn't sure what Peter's reaction would be, and he'd been ready to back away when he got one of Peter's radiant, dimpled smiles. "Wow."

"Yeah, I'd say so." The seat crunched beneath him as Russ settled, looking out the windshield at the back of Peter's garage with all the tools leaning haphazardly against the walls. *So unlike Barry in all the best ways possible.* "I think we should go inside."

Peter nodded, and Russ heard the trunk release pop before Peter opened his door. Russ got out the chair and then left Peter to transfer himself into it while he brought in the boxes. "I just have one thing to ask," Russ said as he set the last box beside the kitchen table as Peter had requested. "Are there baby pictures of you in these boxes?" Russ couldn't help asking, and he saw the look of fear on Peter's face.

"God, I hope not!" Peter was mortified, and Russ nearly started digging through the boxes himself but settled for a devious grin.

"I bet you were a beautiful baby." Russ lifted one of the boxes and set it on Peter's lap before looking at him expectantly. Russ half expected Peter to balk, but he opened the box and began looking through it.

"It's just a bunch of my old school papers," he explained before maneuvering the box onto the table. "That's probably what they all are."

"Do you want me to put them somewhere for you?" Russ asked.

"No. I'll go through them when I have a chance," Peter said. "Get yourself a beer if you'd like one."

Russ turned to go to the refrigerator, knocking the top box off the stack. It fell on its side, and what looked like things from Peter's childhood spilled onto the floor. Russ bent to start picking things up, smiling when he handed Peter what looked like an old clay ashtray. "You made one of these too?"

"Yeah," Peter said taking it from Russ. "Mom kept everything." Russ continued picking up the spilled contents of the box. "Stop," Peter called. "Please. What's that envelope? It looks like my mother's handwriting." Russ reached to where Peter was indicating and handed him an envelope with his name on it, and Peter took it, handling it like it was a holy relic. Peter turned the envelope in his hand, looking at the front and back before staring at the front again. "Where did this come from?"

"Isn't it part of your stuff?"

Peter shook his head. "I've never seen it before." Peter opened the envelope and pulled out what looked like two pieces of notebook paper. Russ finished picking up the things he'd spilled and set the box down before getting a beer from the fridge. When he turned around, Peter was holding the papers, staring at them in what looked like total disbelief.

"What's wrong?" Russ got up and stood behind Peter's chair, lightly touching his shoulders. "Are you okay?" Peter didn't move other than to shift the papers in his hands and continue reading. As Russ watched, he cycled through the papers again and again, rereading them over and over, as though he could not believe what was written on them. "Peter, what is it?"

Peter shook his head, and Russ stroked his shoulders as he heard the papers rustle yet again. He had no idea what could be on them, and he purposely gave Peter his privacy. But the longer he acted like this, the more Russ became concerned. "I can't believe this," Peter finally said, and Russ breathed a small sigh.

"Is there anything I can do?" Russ asked, having no idea at all what was wrong.

"No. I don't think so." Peter didn't look away from the papers.

"Do you want me to go?" Russ asked, and he lifted his hands away from Peter's shoulders. Peter shook his head, but didn't say anything more. "You're scaring me, Peter."

Finally Peter set the pages on the table and looked at Russ, but he couldn't say anything. It was then Russ saw the lines of tears running down Peter's cheeks, and he leaned forward, hugging Peter tightly. At first Peter didn't move, but then Russ felt Peter's arms tighten around him, hugging him silently. Russ still wondered what had upset Peter, but he didn't feel as though he had the right to pry, and if what Peter wanted was comfort, then he'd give it to him for as long as he wanted.

"Do you want to talk about it? I'll listen if you do?"

Peter shook his head. "There's nothing you can do." Peter released him from the hug and sat back in his chair. "I don't think there's anything anyone can do."

"Is the letter really from your mother?" Russ asked, and Peter nodded slowly, reaching to pick up the pages and handing them to Russ.

CHAPTER FIVE

PETER could barely get any air into his lungs. He felt as though someone were sitting on his chest. Papers rustled, and he knew Russ was reading the letter from his mother, the woman who'd wiped his tears and patched scraped elbows, the woman who'd always been the loudest voice in the cheering section every time he raced. She was the one who'd comforted him when the doctors gave him the news that he would never walk again. And yet, two sheets of handwritten notebook paper had changed everything and made him wonder if he'd known her at all.

"Peter," Russ said softly, a hand resting on his shoulder. Reaching up, he took the sheets and placed them on the table. He wanted to destroy them, rip the pages to shreds and along with them the words that shocked and hurt. "You didn't know." Peter shook his head and swallowed hard, trying to reconcile everything he knew about his mother with what she'd told him, or more precisely, had never told him. "Peter, it's okay."

"How could she?" Peter asked to no one in particular as his nose ran and tears leaked out of his eyes. "How could she never tell me?"

"I don't know," Russ said, and Peter turned around slowly, the wheels of his chair not wanting to move. Russ leaned close, and Peter remembered he had the brakes on, and then he was moving out of the kitchen, away from what she'd written. In the living room, he stopped in his usual place in front of the television, but stared at nothing. "What can I do?" Russ asked, and Peter shrugged. There was nothing anyone could do.

"I'll be okay," Peter said automatically, wishing he could ask her why she hadn't told him. Hadn't she loved him enough to tell him? Closing his eyes, Peter blocked out everything until all he could hear was the sound of his own heartbeat in his ears.

"Do you know what this means?" Russ asked, and Peter turned and glared at him.

"Of course I do. It means my mother didn't love me enough or trust me enough to tell me that she'd been pregnant before she was married. That...." Peter stared at Russ, watching him settle on the sofa next to him.

"Peter, it means you have a half-sister, somewhere," Russ said calmly—too calmly.

"But why didn't she tell me?" He had no idea why, but he felt as though part of his life were collapsing.

"I don't know. Maybe your dad knows and can tell you. She must have had a good reason." Russ made it seem so reasonable, but it wasn't. Peter had always told his mother everything, even the hard stuff. He'd told her he was gay long before he told his dad. When he was scared or needed someone to talk with, it had always been her. He'd trusted her with so much, and she had kept her own secrets all that time.

Peter snapped his head to look at Russ, his anger taking over. "What reason could she have had? She lied to me!" Peter saw Russ flinch, and he lowered his eyes.

"Do you want me to go? You have things you need to think through." Russ stood up and walked by his chair. Peter almost let him go, but he had the strangest feeling that if he let Russ walk out now, he'd regret it somehow.

Reaching out, Peter took Russ's hand. "I wasn't yelling at you."

"I know," Russ said, but Peter could see he was still hurt, but he didn't let go of Peter's hand. "Peter, everyone has secrets. You do, I do. Sometimes we bury them so deeply that we begin to forget about them too. Especially when it's something we aren't proud of. And if you think about it, at the time your mom got pregnant outside of marriage, that was still a huge deal, and I bet she wasn't given much choice from her family. So she had the child, gave it up for adoption, and buried the memories and hurt as deeply as she could. I'm willing to bet that she probably agonized over how to tell you and ended up writing the letter in case she could never bring herself to do it."

"How do you know?" Peter knew he was grasping at straws.

"I don't. There's only one person who might, though, and that's your dad," Russ said.

A thought chilled Peter to the core. "What if he doesn't know, either?" Peter saw Russ shiver, and his mouth opened, but nothing came out. "That's exactly how I feel." Russ let go of his hand, and Peter felt the loss almost immediately as he watched Russ go to the window.

"You could call your dad," Russ offered up, still staring outside.

"No. I can't. Not now. I'm too keyed up and I'd say something wrong and hurt him too." Peter moved closer to where Russ stood. "Thanks for being here."

Russ turned, and Peter saw in Russ's eyes his own hurt reflected back at him. "Do you need anything?"

Peter nodded and held out his hand. "I don't want to be alone."

Russ nodded and continued holding his hand for a while. When Russ did let go, it was to get his cell phone. Russ stepped away, and Peter heard him talking on the phone in the other room. "I called Billy and told him I'd be home in the morning," Russ said as he shoved his phone in his pocket. "Do you have some blankets? I can sleep on the sofa."

Peter felt sort of dazed, and he nodded before gliding down the hall to the linen closet. Placing a sheet and blanket on his lap, he backed up and closed the door before gliding back to the sofa. "Thank you for doing this. I know it sounds stupid, but I feel really alone right now."

"It's okay. Be sure to leave your door open. Call me if you need anything, and I'll be right there," Russ said as he began making up a bed on the sofa. Peter watched him for a while before saying good night.

In the bathroom, he cleaned up and left out a new toothbrush and toiletries before gliding across the hall to his bedroom. He left the door partway open as he got undressed, placing his dirty clothes in the basket on the floor of his closet. Like he always did, Peter then got into bed and made sure the chair was within easy reach before turning off the light.

In the darkness, he could hear Russ walk down the hall. Water ran in the bathroom, the toilet flushed, and then it was quiet for a while until he heard the door open and saw the light switch off. The footsteps sounded back down the hall until Peter heard the couch squeak lightly under Russ's weight, then quiet. The entire time Russ had been cleaning up, Peter had been imagining what he'd look like, and now he was imagining Russ lying on the sofa. He didn't know what he was wearing as he slept, but in his mind, Russ was in just a pair of briefs. A small squeak reached Peter's ears, and he imagined Russ rolling over, the blankets slipping off because it was hot. Closing his eyes, he tried to fall asleep.

Peter woke with a start. He'd been dreaming about his mother, and in his dream he'd been calling her a liar every time she said anything. She kept trying to explain, but he kept yelling at her and wouldn't listen. "Peter, are you okay?" Russ asked from his doorway, and Peter focused his eyes to see him. "You were talking in your sleep."

"I... I'm okay," Peter answered, and Russ turned away, his dark form leaving the doorway. "Russ," he said softly, almost too softly, and at first he didn't think Russ had heard him.

"What is it?" Russ whispered. Peter wasn't quite sure, so he stared at Russ, wondering what he did want. That wasn't right, he knew what he wanted, he just wasn't sure if he should ask for it. Then Russ moved closer, and Peter held his breath. "Are you all right?" Peter took Russ's hand and held it. Everything seemed disjointed and out of place, like he was seeing things through a mist. Tugging lightly, Peter felt Russ climb on the bed. He seemed to be moving slowly, like he wasn't sure what Peter wanted, so Peter pushed back the covers, and Russ climbed into bed with him. "Is this really okay?"

As an answer, Peter pulled Russ closer, and the other man held him tight. Peter carefully rolled onto his side, and Russ moved right behind him, spooning him. It had been so long since he'd been held that he barely remembered what it felt like. Before the accident, Peter was the one who usually held his bed partners, but now it felt so good to be held, he couldn't describe it.

"Russ," Peter whispered in the dark.

"Yeah."

"Is that…?"

"Sorry." Russ shifted the position of his hips.

"Don't be."

Russ's hips returned, and Peter shifted backward a little, smiling. And if Russ had checked, he would have found that Peter was in the exact same condition. But Russ's hands remained firmly tucked around Peter's middle and showed no signs of moving, so Peter closed his eyes and let himself fall asleep. His dreams weren't much calmer than they had been, but whenever he woke up, Russ was there, holding him tight.

In the morning, Peter woke sweaty and hot, with Russ pressed to his back. The covers were gone and Russ was holding him just like he had all night. "You awake?" Russ asked quietly in his ear, and Peter nodded. "Feeling any better?" Peter shook his head. All night long, he kept wondering why his mother hadn't told him and if his father knew. Sometime during the night, he'd tried to tell himself that his father must know, but then that meant both of them had kept this from him. "You know it's okay to be hurt and angry."

"Well, I am that," Peter deadpanned.

Russ sighed behind him, and Peter turned his head to look into Russ's deep eyes. "You know this isn't about you. It's really about your mom." Peter groaned and tried to roll away, but Russ held him firmly. "She had a baby and she had to give it up. That must have been painful as hell. Do you talk about all the painful things in your life all the time?"

"No," Peter had to admit, even though he didn't want to concede that Russ was right.

"She wanted to move on, and yet she did want you to know, hence the letter, so cut her a little slack. She was still your mom and she always loved you, no matter what. This doesn't change that." Russ leaned forward, and Peter relaxed and let himself be kissed. "It doesn't change anything except the fact that now you know. It's like coming out. When I told my friends I was gay, they all asked me when I decided that. I told them I didn't decide to be gay. My only decision was to tell them. Yes, your mother probably should have told you in person, and instead you saw it in a letter after she was gone, but would you rather not know at all?" Russ rubbed his stomach lightly, and Peter moved into the gentle touch, closing his eyes.

"You make it sound so reasonable," Peter said with his eyes closed.

"Because maybe it is." Russ kissed him again, and Peter felt Russ's hand slip down his stomach. Silently, behind his closed eyes, he hoped Russ kept going and took the step he so desperately wanted him to take. His entire body ached, and Peter was two seconds from begging when Russ's hand stopped and fell away. Peter cracked his eyes open, wondering what had happened. Russ stared back at him with a small smile. "I think we should get up," Russ told him, but he made no effort to move away. "I know what you want, and I want it too." Russ looked down the bed, and Peter followed his eyes, because evidence of what Peter wanted was tenting the sheet.

Peter leaned forward to kiss Russ softly. "But you're not ready," Peter finished for him, and Russ nodded.

"I know it sounds kind of dumb, but I want to be sure. You deserve more than just sex."

"No. I don't," Peter said, pouting his lips.

Russ chuckled and kissed him one more time. Afterward, he slowly got out of bed. "I know you don't need help getting out of bed, but is there something I can do to make it easier?"

"I can get it." Peter tried to keep the disappointment out of his voice.

"Okay," Russ said before leaving the room. Peter sat up and worked his way toward the chair, scooting himself off the bed and onto the seat. "I just need a little more time," Russ said from the hallway.

"I know, and I shouldn't have pushed," Peter said as he rolled out of the bedroom and found himself sitting in front of Russ.

"Peter." Russ leaned close, his hands on the arms of the chair. "We've each been through a lot. I just want to make sure this is right before we take that step. I need to."

Peter sighed and looked away. "I know being with someone who can't use his legs takes a bit of getting used to."

Russ rolled his eyes. "Please. The feeling-sorry-for-myself act is a little unattractive. Remember I see you, not the chair." Peter felt Russ's fingers under his chin. "Your being in a wheelchair doesn't matter shit to me, but you feeling sorry for yourself is a bit off-putting." Russ stared deep into Peter's eyes, and he couldn't look away, no matter how much he wanted to. "Do you know when you're at your most handsome?" Peter shook his head. "When you're flying around that track like no one can catch you. You look like you're on the top of the world."

Russ's expression changed, and he hurried away without saying anything more. Peter heard rustling sounds in the living room, and then Russ hurried back and placed a piece of paper in his hand. "There's a club that meets at the school once a week. It's a wheelchair racing club. They meet Sunday afternoons, and since I'm off today I thought, if you wanted, I'd go with you."

Russ looked so excited, and Peter stared at the paper in his hands. "I'm not sure I'm good enough."

"Yeah, right. You were flying around the track, dude. What have you got to lose?" Russ's eyes twinkled with excitement, and Peter found himself agreeing to give it a try. After getting another kiss, Russ hurried away to get dressed, and Peter went into the bathroom to take care of things.

Once he was dressed, they left the house, and Peter drove Russ to Billy and Darryl's, dropping him off. Russ agreed to meet him at the school track at two, in time for the club meeting, and Peter watched him bound into the house before heading back home to make the dreaded phone call to his dad.

PETER pulled into the parking lot of the school and waited to see if anyone actually showed up. Russ hurried over to the car and pulled the door open almost before Peter put the car in park. "How did it go with your dad?"

"I don't know. I mentioned the letter, and he clammed up tight, so I'm sure he knows what happened to Mom, but he refused to talk about it at all. Every time I brought it up, he changed the subject, and when I pressed directly, he said he was late for something at the church, told me a hurried goodbye, and hung up." Peter sighed, and Russ opened the back door, pulling out Peter's racing chair and moving it into place by the car door. "I don't know about this," Peter said nervously. His stomach jumped as he saw three or four men wheeling themselves toward the track.

"What are you afraid of? That they'll pick on you and call you names like 'Wheelie Boy' or tell you that your chair is 'so last week, dude'?" Russ's imitation of a surfer made him laugh, and he transferred himself to the chair, letting Russ close the door as he guided himself toward the track. He heard Russ following behind and saw some of the other guys looking his way. "I brought a book and I'm going to sit in the shade," Russ told him, holding up a paperback, and he veered off with a small wave. Peter watched him go before continuing on his way to join the group.

"Hi, I'm Ty," one of the guys said as he approached, and Peter saw him looking over Peter's chair.

"Peter Christopoulos," he said, introducing himself to the group.

"This is Bill"—Ty began pointing to each of the other guys— "Mark, Skip, Phil, and Ronnie. Have you raced before?"

Peter shook his head. "I've been on the track, but always alone."

"A newbie, huh?" Ty smiled. "We meet once a week while the weather's good, and the rest of the year we try to get together to keep active." Ty picked up the clipboard hooked to the side of his chair. "How did you find us?"

"A friend," Peter said, gesturing in Russ's direction, "found you on the Internet."

Ty smiled. "We're glad you came," he said, and the other guys nodded, some of them reaching out to shake Peter's hand. "Right now we're training for a team competition next month." Ty set down his clipboard. "Let's warm up, okay? And Skip, this isn't a race, just a warm-up."

Peter watched as the man in question hurried toward the track. "Skip hates to lose at anything, even warm-ups," Ronnie said from next to him, and Peter chuckled, following the others. They made a leisurely circuit of the track, and Peter could feel his muscles loosening. Skip had already taken off and made his complete lap before anyone else got three-quarters of the way around. Peter took his time and followed the others.

"We're timing today," Ty said as they all gathered at the end of the track. "We'll go in groups of two. Plan to make at least two runs, hopefully three," Ty said, and the others nodded. Peter looked at him for an explanation. "Each race is three laps. We're just going for timings, so all you really want to do is beat your own time, unless you're Skip, who has to beat everyone's," Ty ribbed the other racer, but he didn't seem to pay attention. "Since you're so all fired up, you and Mark can go first, that way Peter can watch."

"Okay, Mark, are you ready to eat my dust?" Skip taunted as he lifted his chair onto the back wheels, balancing until he got into position. Ty started them, and both men took off, arms pumping, with Skip jumping ahead and staying there the entire race. When they crossed the line, Ty called out each man's time and wrote it on his board. Ronnie and Ty went next, with Phil starting them and keeping time. Both Ty and Ronnie beat Mark's time, but Skip's was the best so far, and he hollered and razzed all the guys about it.

When it was his turn, Peter wheeled himself onto the track with Phil. "Just do your best," Phil told him, but Peter was more worried about making a fool of himself. He looked over at the tree and saw Russ stand up. Ty called out, and Peter's concentration focused on the race. "Go!"

Peter propelled his chair forward, moving faster and faster, just like he had when he was alone. Peter had already determined that he wasn't going to look for Phil, but just do what he always did: make himself go as fast as he could. At the edge of his consciousness, he heard people calling out and yelling, but they barely intruded on his concentration. One lap, then two, and by the third his arms were stoked and he added more weight to his pumping, gaining still more speed.

"Yes, that's it!" he heard Ty cry, and Peter stopped pumping, letting the chair coast to a stop. Looking around, he wondered if he'd disgraced himself. That is, until he heard Russ yelling and running over to him, and he looked back and saw that Phil still had half a lap to go.

"I knew you could do this!" Russ shouted as he caught up with him. "You did it!"

Peter smiled, and Russ high-fived him before they both made their way back to where the others were waiting for him. Phil finished, and Peter grinned when Ty gave him his time. "You were just a few seconds slower than Skip. If you'd have put on that speed earlier, you'd have killed him." Ty grinned at him, and Skip scowled for a few seconds before smiling and reaching over to shake Peter's hand.

"Cool, dude. You can really move."

"We'll take five and then go again," Ty said, obviously pleased. "Are you serious about doing this? Because you've got real speed and control."

"Yeah, I think so. I've been training on my own for health reasons for almost a year, but it was fun to race against someone."

"Do you want to go to Central Penn regionals in six weeks? The team's a man short and we could use you." Ty sounded really excited.

"I think I'd like that. Can I let you know?"

"You coming back next week?" Skip asked, once again balancing on his back wheels.

"If you'll have me," Peter answered, looking at all the guys and seeing them nod. "Then can I let you know about regionals next week?"

"Of course," Ty said, but Peter could tell he wanted an answer, and that he wanted Peter to go. "Second heat," Ty said, and they raced again. Skip's time improved, and so did Peter's, although not quite enough to beat him, but he was close again. By the third heat, Peter's time increased again, and this time he did beat Skip, earning the fastest time. And with every heat, Peter could hear Russ nearly yelling himself hoarse.

After the races, Peter was tired and his arms ached, but he felt invigorated and excited. Wheeling himself to where the other racers had congregated, Peter gave Ty his contact information, and after talking about the highs and lows of the practice, they all headed back to their cars. Once the guys began to leave, Russ hurried over and engulfed Peter in a huge hug. "You were great. You flew around the track and you beat everybody! You're not mad at me for pushing you into this, are you?"

"No. It was fun and I loved it." One of the side benefits was that he hadn't thought about his mom or the letter the entire time. All he'd thought about was racing, his body, and the way Russ cheered him on. "Let's go home. I need to clean up, and then we can get some food. I'm starved."

Peter glided toward his car, and Russ walked with him. Once Peter got into the car, Russ put his chair behind the seat, and he leaned against the door, looking into the open driver's side window. "See, I was right."

"About what?" Peter asked.

"You are sexiest when you're racing." Russ winked at him before stepping back from the car.

Peter chewed on his lower lip, wanting to ask, but not sure if he should. "Do you want to come back to the house?" He swallowed, lifting his gaze from a fascinating speck of dirt on the paint up to Russ's eyes. "You...."

Russ leaned closer again, and Peter's eyes drifted closed as Russ kissed him through the open window. "Okay. I have a stop to make, though."

"I should get cleaned up," Peter said, already thinking about how he wanted to look when Russ arrived. Other than for work, he hadn't worried about his clothes in a while, but he wanted to look his best for Russ. "Is half an hour okay?"

Russ smiled one of those smiles that made his eyes crinkle. "Perfect." Russ kissed him again quickly before standing back so Peter could raise the window. As he turned onto the street, Peter noticed Russ walk back toward his car.

Peter hurried home and got himself undressed and into the shower as quickly as he could, which for him meant that, after the ten-minute drive home, it took him the rest of the half hour just to get undressed, showered, and dressed again. There were times that being him drove him crazy, and this was one of them. Combing his hair, Peter even sprayed on a little cologne before wheeling himself into the kitchen, where he located a bottle of white wine and placed it in the fridge to chill. He was probably jumping to conclusions and getting his hopes up, but he didn't care. Peter felt excited, and not just sexually, although that was nice too.

Checking the clock again, Peter rolled into the living room and peered out the window. He half expected to see Russ pulling into the driveway, but it was empty. Figuring Russ was running behind, he turned on the television and began to watch one of the competitive cooking shows that were becoming so popular. The contestant everyone loved to hate was just spouting off about how he was going to kick sweet, quiet Anna's culinary butt when Peter heard a car pull into the driveway. Looking up, Peter was surprised to see it wasn't Russ's car, but his father's.

Peter felt a jolt of anxiety shoot through him. As he turned off the television, he heard his father come in the back door. "I'm in the living room, Dad," Peter called, and he heard his father's footsteps come through the house. "I wasn't expecting you," Peter said, glancing at the driveway before turning toward his father.

"We cannot talk about this on the phone, and I hoped you would be home," his dad said, sitting uncomfortably in one of the chairs.

"So you did know," Peter said, his mind immediately shifting back to what he'd read in his mother's letter, the feelings of hurt and betrayal that he'd pushed aside rushing back.

"Yes. I knew, but it was not my story to tell. And after your mother died, I saw no need to bring it up. What happened was long ago and in her past. I did not know that she wrote a letter. Where did you find it?" His father remained on the edge of the chair.

"It was in a book that was in one of the boxes you gave me. Mom remembered that *The Count of Monte Cristo* was one of my favorite stories, and I think she placed the letter in the book. The box fell and things got scattered, but that's my best guess," Peter said, not feeling comfortable at all. He glanced out the window again and then back to his dad. "What I can't figure out is why neither of you told me. I have a half-sister somewhere, and neither of you said anything." Peter tried unsuccessfully to keep the hurt out of his voice.

"I will explain, but you must know that this has nothing to do with you or how much your mother loved you," his father said with a touch of frustration and hurt in his voice.

"She didn't love me enough to tell me," Peter snapped, and his father jumped to his feet, glaring at him with hard eyes.

"Your mother loved you enough to try to spare you her shame and hurt," his father hissed, and Peter leaned back in his chair as his father's expression softened slightly. "Before we were married, your mother was engaged to a man who she thought she was in love with. I knew Nico and hated him because he had your mother's eye. She was about twenty and thought Nico was going to marry her, so she fell for his pretty words and soft expressions. To make a long story short, he got her pregnant, and when he found out, he left in a hurry." Peter's father sank back into the chair. "Your grandfather shipped your mother off to live with relatives as soon as she started to show, until the baby was born. Then he forced your mother to give the girl up for adoption. It nearly killed your mother, but she did it because that was what she thought she was supposed to do."

"Did you know Mom had had a baby when you married her?" Peter asked, most of his own anger and hurt seeping away when he heard about his mother's. But that didn't stop him from glancing once again out the window and wondering where Russ was.

"Are you expecting someone?" his father asked shortly.

"Russ was coming over," Peter answered before returning his attention to his dad.

"To answer your question, I did know. But I'd loved your mother ever since I'd first seen her and it didn't matter to me. But the loss of her baby hurt your mother, and it wasn't until we had you that she seemed completely herself again. She had a child to love, and the memory of the one she'd given up faded, I believe. Then she had your sister." His father smiled very briefly. "When we lost Diane, I thought I was going to lose your mother too, because she was feeling the loss of both of her daughters. She never talked about the child she gave up, but I know she felt double the pain." Peter saw what he thought might have been a tear in his father's eyes. Peter had only seen his father cry one time, and that was at his mother's funeral.

"Why didn't she tell me, Dad?" Peter blinked back his own threatening tears.

"She told no one. I tried to talk about it, but your mother would hear nothing of it. She refused to speak about it to anyone." Costa wiped his eyes with his hand, and Peter heard his dad steady his breath before continuing. "A few years after Diane's death, I found out by accident that your mother had been looking for the child she'd given up. When I confronted her, she said that she hadn't been able to find her, and that was the last we ever talked about it."

"She said the same thing in the letter," Peter told his dad. "She also said that she never tried to find her again." Peter tried to imagine the pain and anguish his mother had felt when she learned that her child was truly lost to her. "I think I know when that happened." He remembered coming home from school to find his mother still in bed when he was about ten, and she'd stayed there for almost three days. It was the only time he could remember his mother acting like that.

"Looking back, you probably do," his father agreed, nodding slowly. "I think failing probably hurt too much, and she couldn't bear to fail again." His father stood up and walked to where Peter sat. "Never doubt that your mother loved you, just as I never doubt that she loved me. The loss of this daughter hurt your mother terribly, and if I could have made it go away, I would have. You know your mother could be as stubborn as they come, and in this she would not budge. The only time she ever talked about it, she told me that she'd made one mistake on top of the other, but that neither you nor I should have to pay for it, so she buried her hurt deep and loved both of us with everything she had."

"Why did she write the letter?" Peter asked, and his father shrugged and shook his head.

"I don't know, and I doubt we ever will. Towards the end, she had moments of complete clarity, and then spent days where she didn't know who she was. I can only guess that by then, she wanted you to know, but couldn't manage or wasn't able to tell you. I'm afraid the real answer to that question died with her."

Peter nodded and sat staring at his father, thoughts swirling through his head. Should he try to find her? Did he really want to find his half-sister? Did she want to be found? Peter's head throbbed, and he held it with his hands.

"I know what you're thinking, and the decision to find her is up to you. I promised your mother I would never try, but you aren't bound by that promise." His father patted his shoulder lightly. "I'll support whatever you decide, but think about it before you do anything."

"I will, Dad," he promised, placing his hand on his father's. A sound from outside drew Peter's attention, and he saw Russ's car pull into the driveway. When he turned back to his father, he saw him staring at him.

"You really like him, don't you?" his father asked as he moved away to sit back down.

"Yes, Dad, I do," Peter answered, the expression on his father's face confusing him.

"He's been hurt. When he didn't think I was looking, I saw the same pain in his eyes that your mother tried to hide from me." Sometimes his dad surprised the socks off Peter, and this was one of those times. He wondered how much he should tell his father, and decided on the bare minimum.

"His last partner was abusive," Peter told his dad, and he saw his skeptical expression. "I saw the bruises." His father's eyes widened, and Peter didn't go into anything more as he heard a soft knock on the front door. Peter glided over and unlocked the door before opening it.

"I'm sorry I'm late," Russ said as he stepped inside, carrying a bag. "Oh, Costa," he said, seeing Peter's dad, and he then turned back to Peter. "I can come back, or…."

"No, we were just talking," Peter explained as lightly as he could.

"I should go," his dad said as he stood up and walked toward the door. "I have things to do." Peter's dad hugged him goodbye and shook Russ's hand before leaving the house and walking to his car.

"I didn't mean to interrupt," Russ said as he set the bag on the sofa before closing the door.

"You didn't. We were done," Peter said, feeling a little numb after what his father had told him. "He explained what happened with my mom."

"Intense?" Russ asked, kneeling down so he could hug him properly, and Peter returned the hug with joy and relief.

"That's an understatement. The short version is that I have a half-sister out there somewhere. Mom tried to find her years ago, but couldn't." Russ released him from the hug and sat on the sofa near him, still holding Peter's hand. "Dad said it broke her heart and she carried the guilt and loss with her until she died."

Russ nodded. "Are you still angry with her?"

"I guess. I'm not sure what I feel about all this. I wish she would have told me when she was alive." Peter's thoughts were still going in multiple directions, and he felt like he was strapped to a teeter-totter, going back and forth without ever getting anywhere. "But I sort of understand why she didn't want to talk about it." Peter humphed softly. "I don't know what the hell to think."

"That's sort of what I figured, so I brought some movies and junk food. I sort of figured we could watch something and eat. 'Cause, after all, nothing says comfort like cookies and men wearing next to nothing." Russ dangled a DVD of *Troy* in front of Peter's face. "The movie's okay, but Brad Pitt, Eric Bana, and Orlando Bloom spend a lot of it running around shirtless, and there are even a few flashes of butt if you look close." Russ waggled his eyebrows, and Peter couldn't help chuckling.

"How did you know I needed this?"

"I didn't. I figured we could watch movies and stuff if you wanted. It was just a lucky coincidence that I stopped to get the junk food." Russ set the bag aside and sat back on the sofa, and Peter moved his chair and set the brakes, shifting onto the sofa as well. Russ got up to put in the DVD and then sat back down. As soon as the movie started, Russ moved closer to him, an arm around his shoulder, and Peter rested his head on Russ's shoulder, letting the thoughts about his mother fade to the background for now.

By the time Achilles and Hector were having their epic sword fight, Peter had decided what he wanted to do and finally let himself just enjoy the movie, but he didn't remember much more of it. He woke in time to see the storming of Troy, Russ's arms wrapped around him. They'd sort of shifted on the sofa, with Peter resting his head on Russ as his pillow. Thankfully, Russ didn't seem to mind. By the time the move ended a short time later, Peter had completely lost interest, since Russ was kissing him, and he could have cared less about who lived or died in the movie.

Russ reached around him and used the remote to turn off the television before once again taking Peter's mouth in a kiss that threatened to switch off his brain. Every fiber of Peter's being silently begged for Russ to go for more and not stop. Every time Russ came up for air, Peter held his breath waiting to see if this would end.

As Russ lifted Peter's head and stood up, he did his best and failed to stifle the groan that began in his toes. Russ grabbed a small pillow from one of the chairs and placed it on the end of the sofa before positioning Peter's head on it. Peter watched as Russ moved in slow motion, straddling his body before kissing him hard. Peter pulled Russ closer to him, and he stopped, peering down into Peter's eyes. "I don't want to hurt you," Russ said softly.

"I'm not a doll," Peter answered, and he tightened his hug, holding Russ to him as they went back to kissing. Russ tasted like cookies and beer followed by warmth and sunshine. Peter felt himself shivering with excitement as Russ kept kissing, his lips tugging and nibbling on Peter's.

It had been so long, Peter could barely remember what to do, but Russ definitely seemed to know. Hell, Russ was a master kisser, so much so that Peter barely noticed that his shirt had been untucked until Russ's hand moved beneath it to stroke his stomach. "Is this okay?" Russ asked, moving his hand higher, lightly plucking one of Peter's nipples.

"Okay?" Peter rasped. "Don't you dare stop." Peter pulled Russ into another kiss, and Russ kept stroking his skin. Until that moment, Peter had not realized just how badly he missed being touched. People had hugged him, and he'd been poked and prodded by doctors with the coldest hands on earth for months, but no one had touched him this way, intimately. He had people who loved him, Peter knew that, but to feel someone's hands on his skin and their lips on his to make him feel special was almost like awakening from a three-year sleep. Every fiber of his being reveled in Russ's touch and screamed out for more.

"Can I?" Russ asked, and Peter sat up slightly. As soon as he did, Russ tugged off Peter's shirt and wrapped his arms around Peter's waist, holding him upright. Peter's own high-pitched moan filled the room as Russ's tongue swirled around one of his nipples.

"Russ," Peter whined when he felt him sucking lightly on his skin. Peter wanted more, and he wanted some relief from the throbbing tightness in his pants.

"You like that?" Russ asked with a sly grin before sucking on the other nipple without waiting for an answer, his warm hands stroking up and down Peter's sides. "I love how soft and beautiful your skin is," Russ told him as he kissed trails over Peter's chest. "So rich." Russ licked a long line up one of Peter's sides, then over to a nipple before continuing on to the base of Peter's neck. "I've wondered what you'd taste like since I first saw you roll into the restaurant." Russ's hands caressed along Peter's back, fingers splaying along his muscles.

"Me too," Peter mumbled, his head falling back as Russ went back to work, doing the most amazing things to his nipples. Panting softly, Peter clamped his eyes closed and let Russ take him on a sensual journey. Each touch seemed to fire every nerve in his body, and every time Russ's hands did that thing where they skirted just above his belt, he felt as though he might never be able to catch his breath again. "Please," Peter begged almost under his breath as Russ spent an inordinate amount of time teasing the skin just below his belly button. Lifting his head, Russ met his eyes, and Peter waited. Peter could almost see the conflicted feelings on Russ's face, and he bit his lower lip to keep himself from saying more. Peter closed his eyes. "You don't have to, you know."

Russ stopped moving, and Peter felt a hand stroke his cheek. "It isn't a matter of having to or wanting to, because I do. You're incredible." Russ sat up and moved away, much to Peter's consternation. He wanted to pull him back and beg Russ to keep touching him. "I know it sounds dumb, but I feel like I'm cheating on Barry. I know I'm not, but it sort of feels like I am." Russ sat at the end of the sofa, and Peter propped himself up before moving into a sitting position. "You're a wonderful guy, and I know I should be able to do this. I want to do this with you."

Peter looked at the floor. "You don't have to make excuses. I told you being with someone in a chair can be hard. I understand."

"No, you don't!" Russ's harsh tone surprised Peter. "This has nothing to do with you, the chair, or the fact that you can't walk, because you're what matters, not the rest of it. Barry has me so screwed up I don't know which way to turn." Russ stood up and began pacing. "Do you know what sex was like for us?" Russ continued pacing the floor. "Almost from day one, he told me exactly what to do. He controlled almost everything about our lives. I made no decisions and had almost no say, least of all in the bedroom."

"Is that what you like? Being told what to do, I mean?" Peter asked, because that was not his idea of a relationship.

Russ sighed and stopped pacing. "I don't know what I like. I was never asked what I liked for the last four years. Whenever I tried to ask for something, Barry would tell me that he knew what I needed and he'd give it to me when he was ready. No matter what you think, after a while of being told the same thing again and again, you start to believe it."

Peter held out his hand, and after a few moments, Russ moved closer, taking his hand. "It's okay." Peter felt as relieved as he'd ever been in his life. "Take your time and listen to your heart. When you go to bed at night and fantasize, that's what you like, not what Barry told you was good for you. That was what *he* wanted, not what you wanted. So how about we make a deal?"

"What kind of deal?" Russ asked suspiciously.

Peter stopped himself from smiling. "When it comes to anything important, let's assume that whatever Barry the Bastard said or did was wrong. Part of the abuse was him supplanting your desires and needs with his own, including making you feel guilty for moving on."

Russ chuckled and moved closer. "I think I can live with that."

"Okay," Peter said, grinning. "Then why don't you take off your shirt?" Russ looked at him dubiously but did as Peter asked before standing in front of him.

"What do you want me to do?" Russ asked.

"Whatever you want—you don't need my permission for anything," Peter said softly before stroking along Russ's chest, and he felt the muscles under his hands quiver and shake. Russ moved to the sofa, kneeling on the cushions, and Peter shifted so their bodies were closer. "Your body knows what it wants even if your mind doesn't." Peter leaned forward, his lips touching Russ's skin. Peter almost leaned too far, but Russ caught him and then kissed him.

"Maybe we can move to the bedroom," Russ whispered, and he got up off the sofa, bringing the chair closer. Peter transferred himself to it and let Russ walk him down the hall. Peter never did that if he could help it. He hated being pushed in the chair because it meant he was at someone else's mercy, but he didn't mind Russ doing it now. It felt sort of like foreplay, his equivalent to being led to the bedroom by the hand, especially when Russ lightly squeezed his shoulder, making contact with his skin.

In the bedroom, Peter transferred himself to the bed and let Russ move the chair away. "Look, tonight you take the lead," Peter said as he wrapped his arms around Russ's neck and back, tugging them close together. You can't do anything wrong as long as it's from your heart."

"Are you sure?" Russ asked skeptically.

"Yes, I'm sure." God, he was so sure he was vibrating when Russ laid him back on the bedding and pulled off his pants. Peter hadn't lost all feeling in his legs, just a lot of it, but when Russ touched them, what usually felt like feeling things through mud became sharper and crisper. Peter wasn't sure if that happened because he wanted it to or not, and right now he didn't care. As Russ moved his hands up Peter's legs, the sensation became sharper and stronger, like his hands were coming out of a fog. By the time Russ had reached his hips, Peter was bucking slightly, his briefs totally tented.

Peter hissed when Russ nuzzled his cock through the material, trying to keep himself from blowing right then and there. He felt like a teenager having his first experience all over again. Peter touched Russ's cheeks, guiding him to his lips. "You're an amazing man, Russ." Peter hugged him close, and Russ settled on the bed next to him. It was obvious regardless of what his body said that Russ was not comfortable, and that was paramount to Peter, so he just held him and let everything else go.

"But you… we…," Russ stammered.

"That's not important. We were forcing it." Actually, Peter felt like *he* was forcing it, and he didn't want to do that. "We have all the time in the world, and if we don't make love tonight, we can do it some other time."

"Making love?" Russ echoed softly.

Peter turned his head to peer into Russ's eyes. "That's the only term I can think of to use. When you engage your heart, it's making love. You're not a casual fuck, not to me." Peter held his breath and tried not to sigh as his stomach did a backflip. Maybe he'd judged this all wrong, and Russ didn't feel the way he thought he did. Maybe this was just Russ getting over Barry and nothing more. Maybe Peter was just some rebound guy to help him heal, and then Russ would move on.

"Sounds nice," Russ said softly, and Peter felt him curl closer. "I doubt if Barry and I ever did that the entire time we were together." Russ lapsed into silence lying next to him. "I hate that I keep talking about Barry." Russ lifted his head, and Peter met his gaze. "I'm lying here with you and we're almost naked together, and all I keep talking about is Barry."

Peter nodded; he'd definitely noticed. "He's part of you, whether you like it or not. I'm hoping you just need some time and distance." Peter prayed that was all Russ needed, because his heart was already reaching out to the other man, and getting hurt was not something he looked forward to. Peter kept replaying Russ's words to his dad that he wouldn't purposely hurt him, and Peter clung to that. He really didn't think Russ had a hurtful bone in his body, but what bothered Peter most was the idea that Russ would realize that he wanted more than Peter, someone whole.

"What I need is a backbone transplant," Russ murmured, continuing to look into Peter's eyes. "Sometimes I feel so lost."

"It's only been a matter of days. Give yourself time," Peter advised, for himself as much as Russ. Hugging tighter, Peter stroked along Russ's arm, enjoying the feel of his smooth, soft skin, trying to ignore the fact that his cock continued to strain the cotton of his briefs. Russ's scent filled Peter's nose, and damn if every breath didn't bring a new wave of musky headiness. Peter knew Russ had noticed, and he did his best to try to ignore it as well, hoping his body would take the hint.

Russ moved away and climbed off the bed, walking toward the door. "You're leaving?" Peter asked in disappointment.

"I'm just teasing you by staying here," Russ said, and Peter felt his gaze travel down his body to accentuate his point.

"That will pass," Peter said, referring to his currently excited Mr. Happy. "There are other things besides sex, and simply being together is one of them." Russ moved closer, and Peter fished around on the floor for his pants. "I really don't want you to go." Russ handed Peter his pants, and he went through the gyrations needed to get them on before sliding off the bed and into his chair. Peter rolled toward the living room, where they retrieved their shirts and pulled them on. Peter transferred himself back to the sofa, and Russ sat next to him after putting in another movie. Peter ordered a pizza for a late dinner, and they watched the movie while they waited for it. At first, Russ sat on the far edge of the sofa, saying nothing, but eventually he moved closer, holding Peter's hand. But by the end of the next movie and the pizza, Russ was holding him again. Peter knew he had to be patient and give Russ time.

"I should really get going," Russ said when the movie ended. "I have to help Darryl in the morning before I meet you and the installers." Russ leaned closer and gave Peter a soft kiss. "I feel bad about…."

"Don't," Peter said, touching Russ's lips with a finger. "You have nothing to feel sorry about. You'll know when you're ready, and I shouldn't have pushed. I don't want you to feel bad." Peter hugged Russ tight, hoping things would be all right between them. Russ kissed him again before getting up, and Peter shifted back to his chair and saw Russ to the door. "I'll see you tomorrow at the restaurant," Peter said, and Russ said good night before leaving the house and walking to his car. Peter watched as Russ got inside and drove away. Closing the door, he tried to tell himself that things were going to be all right, but he really believed that he'd blown it.

He really wished he had someone he could talk to, but no one came to mind. Sure, he had friends, but not someone he could talk with about things like this. His phone rang, pulling him out of his thoughts, and Peter picked it up from the coffee table.

"Hi, Dad," he said, "is something wrong?"

"No. I wanted to make sure you were okay." His dad sounded unusually tentative.

"I'm fine. I've had time to think and I think I'm starting to understand. I'm not ready to forgive her for not telling me yet, but I will. It'll take some time." That bit of wisdom he'd been using a lot lately. "I've also decided that I'm going to try to find her, my half-sister."

"Are you sure?" his dad asked.

"Yes," Peter answered definitively. He hadn't been, up till a few minutes ago, but once he said the words, his resolve firmed. "I want to meet her, and I want to give her the chance to know me. She may not want to, and that's up to her, but I want the chance." The line was quiet for a long time.

"I don't want you to be disappointed. Your mother tried to find her and she couldn't," his dad said, and Peter wondered what he was feeling. This had to be unsettling, to say the least.

"I know, Dad. But I think I need to try. When I first read the letter, I wanted it all to go away, but now I think I need to see this through. She deserves to have the opportunity to know where she comes from." Peter's resolve firmed even more, and he heard his dad sigh through the line.

"I'll help any way I can."

"Thanks, Dad," Peter said with a smile before closing the call. Peter's phone dinged as soon as he hung up, telling him he had a message and a missed call.

Retrieving the message, he played it and heard Russ's voice. "I had a great time today and wanted to call to thank you. I'll see you in the morning." The message wasn't much, but Russ's happy tone settled some of Peter's nervousness. Peter deleted the message and returned Russ's call, and they talked about nothing for almost an hour.

"I told my dad that I'm going to search for my half-sister," Peter finally confessed to Russ. "I don't know if I'll have any luck, but I'm going to try."

Russ was quiet for a few seconds. "Is there anything I can do to help?" More of Peter's nerves faded away, and he smiled into the phone.

CHAPTER SIX

RAIN pelted the windows as Russ rode to Café Belgie with Darryl. "You and Peter seem to be hitting it off," Darryl said as they stopped at the corner light.

"Yeah," Russ said, watching the rain gush down the side window.

"I know I'm no Billy in the advice area, but I'll listen," Darryl told him as the light changed, and he proceeded slowly through the intersection, water rushing down the curbs and into the storm drains.

Russ sighed. "Peter and I... last night we were all set and...." *God, why in the hell is this so hard?* "I couldn't do it." He hoped like hell Darryl understood what he meant from that babbling, because he did not want to have to repeat any of it.

"Translation: you and Peter were ready to have sex, and you couldn't. Is that what you said?" Darryl asked, and Russ nodded vehemently. "That's not the end of the world. It happens to everyone, and most people haven't been through what you've been through." Darryl was being so understanding, and Russ knew he was trying to help, but he felt like crap whenever he remembered the way Peter had stared at the floor, and the crack in his voice.

"You didn't see the look on Peter's face. He thought it was that I didn't want to be with him because he's in a chair. I told him it was because I'm so confused and messed up. I think he believed me, but I can't get his hurt look out of my head. Peter's a really interesting guy. He's smart, and you should have seen him at the track yesterday. There's a club of wheelchair racers, and when we went yesterday, Peter beat their fastest guy once. He looked so happy and excited while he was racing. It was totally awesome." Russ nearly bounced in his seat as he remembered how Peter looked as he raced around the track, arms pumping, his whole body thrown into the task.

Darryl scoffed lightly at Russ's animation and then began to laugh as they pulled into the parking lot behind the restaurant. "You've got it bad."

"What?" Russ asked, and Darryl looked at him over the top of imaginary glasses. "Oh."

"The reason you're so excited about the races and so hurt about what happened yesterday is probably because you're falling for him. You want him to be happy." Darryl parked the car, but left it running, the rain coming down in sheets. "That's a good thing."

"Yeah. But what about Barry? He's an asshole, but I still love him in some stupid way, and I can't seem to let go."

Darryl sighed and turned toward him as a clap of thunder rolled outside the car. "If you could just let Barry go, then Peter probably wouldn't care for you."

"That makes no sense!"

"Sure it does," Darryl said levelly. "Peter probably knows that if you could easily walk away from Barry after four years, then you could do the same to him. But you can't, and that makes you different because you really care. Don't beat yourself up over that. But if I can go against what everyone else thinks here, you should talk to Barry, with someone else present, if necessary. But talk to him—even if it's to yell at him. Just get your feelings out. Let him hear it, and then you can hear what he has to say. You may not like it, but maybe you can put some of this behind you." The rain let up, and Darryl turned off the engine.

"I'll think about it," Russ said, and then they both opened their doors and made a dash for the back door of the restaurant.

The rain might have let up, but they were still nearly soaked by the time they got inside. They stomped their feet on the mat, and Darryl got some towels from the employee restroom so they could dry themselves before turning on the fans and equipment. After changing into their work clothes, they hung their other things in the office and got to work.

Russ helped Darryl with the prep for an hour, until it was time for him to head over to the Acropolis. "There are a few umbrellas in the office," Darryl told him, and Russ gathered his clothes into a bag and got one of the umbrellas before heading out the front door and walking down the sidewalk, where he admitted he really hadn't thought this out when he'd asked Darryl for a ride.

It took about ten minutes, and his shoes were nearly soaked, but the rest of him was dry as he approached the dark restaurant. "Maybe Darryl was right," he said to himself as he looked around for what seemed like the millionth time before unlocking the door. He had to do something. He was tired of looking over his shoulder all the time, wondering if Barry was going to be following him. This had to end.

Walking inside, he closed the umbrella and made sure to place it on the rug before carefully weaving his way to the back door, opening it for the installers, who appeared to be waiting for him. As soon as he opened the door, Russ heard the thunk of truck doors closing and then guys hurried inside, stomping their feet. "Is Peter here?" one of the men asked, and Russ shook his head.

"I expect him anytime."

"We're gonna get to work and should have the last of this installed, but we need to make extra sure you have room for those vertical grills, so we need to take a last set of final measurements before doing the final installation."

"I'll send him back as soon as I see him," Russ promised, and the three men began opening toolboxes and turning on work lights. By the time Russ left, the zing of a drill could already be heard as they got to work. Russ went into the dining area to check the plans for himself. He heard the front door open and turned, expecting to see Peter. Instead, Barry stood in the doorway.

Russ tensed and stared. His first instinct was to back away, but somehow he held his ground. Barry walked closer without saying a word, his eyes resembling those of a feral cat, large and predatory. "What do you want, Barry?" Russ said as levelly as his pounding heart and dry throat would allow. He didn't get a verbal answer, but Barry continued walking closer, and Russ determined he was going to stand his ground. "Why did you come here?"

His question was ignored again, and Barry was now so close, Russ wanted to turn and run into the kitchen where the workmen were. Barry's arms tugged on Russ's shirt and then pulled him tight against Barry's body. Without further warning, Russ was being kissed, hard and full. At first, he was shocked, but as Barry's kiss continued, Russ realized that he felt nothing. There was nothing at all. Barry's lips did nothing, and when his tongue pressed for entrance, Russ kept his mouth closed and tried to pull away. A gasp from near the door brought Russ to full realization, and he shoved on Barry's chest with all his strength. He tried to look at Peter, but Barry towered in front of him, blocking off his view of anything but him. "I told you I knew what you wanted," Barry said in what he must have thought was a seductive voice.

Russ could only imagine the betrayal and disappointment Peter must have been feeling, and when Barry pulled him close once again, Russ did the only thing he could. For the first time since he'd known Barry, Russ lashed out. Drawing his hand back, Russ put all his weight behind it, smacking Barry across the face with everything he had. The sharp sound of his hand on Barry's skin filled the room. Barry looked shocked, and he rubbed his cheek with his hand, eyes wide. "I do not want you to kiss me or do anything else with me," Russ said firmly. He couldn't believe he'd hit Barry, and for a second he felt bad, until he heard laughter. Barry moved aside, and Russ saw Peter laughing to beat the band.

"Take that, Barry the Bastard!" Peter crooned with glee as the workmen filed into the room.

"What happened? Something sounded like a gunshot." Russ did not know the man's name, but he was the biggest and hairiest of the workmen, and Barry took a step back from the huge man. He must have seen the handprint on Barry's face, because the big man looked at Russ and then back at Barry. "Sounds like someone needs to leave his hands at home." Then he turned to Russ. "You need help, just yell."

Russ nodded, and the men glared at Barry before returning to work. "I'm sorry, Peter," Russ said. "I didn't want him to kiss me!" Russ made sure his voice was firm.

"I know," Peter was still chuckling. "So, BB, what is it you wanted?"

Russ turned his attention to his ex. "Yeah, what did you want?"

"I came to talk to you," Barry said rather meekly, which was completely new to Russ.

"You weren't using your lips for talking. So what do you want? Because it's over, Barry. I don't want you to kiss me or try to see me."

"I really came by to talk, and I saw you and—"

"Cut the crap, Barry. You'll say anything to get your own way. What do you want from me? I was with you for four years and put up with all your anal retentiveness." Russ felt all the frustration he'd repressed for years come bubbling to the surface. "You do know that it's not normal to fold your underwear six times and then sort them by color. That's just weird, and let's not get started on your damned closet and fucking shoes. What's worse, you foisted your weirdness on me. So I'll ask again, what is it? You want me to come back so I can sort your socks by color and thread count? What do you want?" Russ glared at Barry, his breath heaving. "I'm waiting for an answer."

"I love you," Barry said.

"I saw the bruises," Peter said from the door. "On his wrists and his back. I also saw the results of your last manhandling the day before Russ left. That's not love, that's abuse, and you need help." Peter sounded determined, and Russ moved to where he sat, standing next to the chair.

"I hope you get the message now. You've spent your last night with me, and you've spent your last breath twisting me around your fingers. We are done, and since I have witnesses, I will call the police, and if you treat anyone the way you treated me, I'll come forward and testify against you. Now I suggest you leave." Russ felt so empowered right now, especially when Barry stepped back. "Go to work, Barry, and find yourself a good therapist." Russ didn't move, and watched until the door closed behind Barry. As soon as it latched, Russ felt his knees buckle from beneath him. Peter tried to catch him, but Russ ended up on the floor regardless, gasping for breath as he tried to process exactly what he'd just done. He'd hit Barry, he'd lashed out at the man who'd controlled almost everything about his life for the better part of four years. Part of him felt like he should be on the top of the world, but another part, the one that had ruled him for the longest time, was scared to death and thought the room started to shake, but after a few seconds he realized it was him.

"You're okay," Russ heard Peter say, and he tried to stand up but couldn't. His legs refused to work, and Russ felt like he might be sick. He felt Peter lightly and gently stroking his back. "Take even breaths and try to relax." Peter's words had less effect on him than his touch. Russ tried to listen, taking careful deep breaths.

"Is he okay?" a deep gruff voice asked, and something in the back of Russ's mind told him it was one of the installers. Russ managed to nod his head, and Peter said something that he didn't really catch. After a few minutes, Russ's head began to clear, and his breathing returned to normal. He tentatively tried to stand, and his legs seemed to stay under him.

"Sorry, I don't know what happened," Russ said, still trying to make sense of things.

"Do you want me to call an ambulance?" Peter asked, his phone already in his hand.

Russ took another deep breath. "No, I'm okay. I just sort of panicked, I guess." Russ looked toward the front door.

"Because he's probably gone for good?" Peter supplied, and Russ nodded, although moving his head made the room jiggle a little even after he'd stopped moving.

"Yeah. There's no going back," Russ said ashamedly. He really didn't want to go back, but the fact that he'd burned his bridges and couldn't go back was scary.

"You know that's another symptom of the abuse. The abuser makes you think you can't get along without them. That's part of the control."

"How do you know so much about this?" Russ asked as he steadied his legs and took a few tentative steps.

"I had a roommate in college who it turned out was an abuser," Peter said, and Russ's eyes widened. "He didn't do anything to me, but his girlfriend was a mess. It took a while for us to see it, but he did the same things to her that Barry did to you. Everything in their relationship was about control, and it was always about Ben controlling Marcy. He followed her to class, made sure he accompanied her wherever she went. At first it looked like he cared enough to protect her because there had been some attacks on women around campus, but it went way beyond that."

Russ listened closely, because that sounded very familiar. He'd first fallen for Barry because he'd been having trouble with the man in the next apartment, and Barry had been protective and caring. "Sounds familiar," Russ mumbled. "What happened?"

Peter shook his head. "She tried more than once to leave, but Ben always pestered her, a lot like Barry did to you, except with more force and determination. She'd leave, and he would woo her with flowers and be all sweet, but as soon as they were together he'd start over again. Ben did to her the same thing Barry did to you. She had fewer and fewer friends, so whenever she tried to leave, her support network was gone. I believe she actually dropped out of school to get away from him. I saw the two of them acting nearly the same as you and Barry, and it's hard, but you have to realize that you're better off being away from him and that you have people who care about you."

Russ sighed loudly and let Peter's words and the caring look on his face sink in. He did have friends, something Barry had tried constantly to keep from happening. "Barry didn't want me to take the job with Darryl," he admitted, and Peter nodded slowly. "He kept saying it was because he would take care of me, but now I see it was because he knew I wouldn't be under his thumb."

"Yup, and it takes a really strong person to do what you did," Peter told him. Russ saw something in his expression he hadn't seen in anyone almost since he was a child. Peter looked proud of him. A loud bang came from the kitchen. Russ jumped, but Peter was already on his way.

Russ couldn't see anything wrong when he entered. "Sorry," one of the guys said. "Part of the hood came loose." He held up a piece of stainless steel. "Didn't hurt anything, just made noise."

Russ nodded and returned to the front of the restaurant as the installers began asking Peter a bunch of questions. He was expecting the tables and chairs anytime, along with some of the other dining room furnishings. Looking out the front window, Russ saw that the rain had stopped. His phone rang just as a large truck pulled up in front. "We're out front with a delivery of tables and chairs."

"Thanks. The front door is open," Russ said, and then he called to Peter to tell him about the delivery. He spent the rest of the morning directing traffic as the tables and chairs were unloaded and placed along one side of what would be the dining area. He was so excited, and having something to keep him busy kept his mind from dwelling on all the crap with Barry. By lunchtime, the delivery men had left. The installers went to lunch, so Russ locked the restaurant and accompanied Peter back to Café Belgie, where they could get something to eat and Russ could let Darryl know about their progress.

AFTER giving Darryl a quick progress report, Russ and Peter took a seat in the Café Belgie dining room, and Billy handed Peter a menu. "I don't think *you* need one," Billy quipped to Russ as he filled their water glasses. They ordered right away and thanked Billy, who hurried off to another table. "So do you have any idea how you're going to find your sister?" Russ asked. He wanted to talk about anything other than the mess with Barry.

"None whatsoever," Peter said. "I wish I knew where to start."

Sebastian's partner, Robert, came in for his usual lunch, and Russ wondered if they could ask him. He was a judge, after all, but Russ wasn't sure if asking him was appropriate or not. Robert seemed to handle that decision when he walked over to their table. "Have you had any more troubles with your ex?" Robert asked.

Peter asked if Robert would like to join them, and he accepted, taking one of the empty chairs. "As a matter of fact," Peter began, "he showed up when we were at the Acropolis this morning, but Russ handled him." Peter winked, and Russ lowered his eyes to the table.

"I just hope he leaves me alone now," Russ said.

"I can put you in touch with someone if you feel you need a restraining order," Robert offered, and Russ thanked him. He was really hoping it wouldn't come to that.

"Actually, there's something Peter might need your advice with," Russ prompted, and Peter explained to Robert what he'd found out.

"We don't want to bother you with this," Peter explained when he'd told Robert about the letter. "But I don't know where to start."

"Things like that can be tricky. The legal system takes a lot into account, including the adopted child's and the adoptive family's right to privacy. To make matters harder, many of those records aren't computerized, so it can take a visit to the courthouse where the adoption was handled, if you know where the adoption was done."

"The only things we know are my mother's name and that the adoption was most likely done in the western portion of the state," Peter explained.

"If you want my opinion, I suggest you hire a good lawyer and have them see what they can find. I've never done that type of work before, and I know it requires a great deal of skill as well as contacts in that area of the state." Robert pulled out his wallet and took a pen from his pocket before writing something on the back of the card and handing it to Peter. "This is a lawyer in Harrisburg who I know has done this sort of thing. He's not cheap, but he's effective, and if anyone can find anything, he can. But I advise you not to get your hopes up. A lot of these cases end up going nowhere or hitting a brick wall because of those privacy and confidentiality issues. A number of things have changed in the last few years, but in Pennsylvania, we tend to cling to older procedures, and this is one of those cases."

Billy brought their lunches and took Robert's order. Sebastian stopped by the table to talk when he had a few minutes, then left and made the rounds of his tables before bringing Robert's lunch.

"I hear you race wheelchairs," Robert said while they ate.

"I'm thinking of joining a club, and they want me to join them in a team race in August, but I've never actually raced anyone for real."

"I think it would be really cool," Russ interjected. "He's really good and unbelievably fast. You should see him."

"Well, if you do decide to race, you need to let us know so we can get together a cheering section," Robert told Peter, and Russ saw the smile on Peter's face. They talked through the rest of their lunch. Robert paid his bill, and after talking with Sebastian for a few minutes, headed back to work.

"I have to call on some clients this afternoon, but if you or the installers have any questions, give me a call on my cell," Peter told Russ on their way back to the Acropolis. "They should be just about done, and once the grills arrive we can complete the installation. The rest of the furnishings for the dining room should arrive next week. When do you expect to begin hiring?"

"Darryl's already started," Russ said as they crossed the main square of town. "Initially, Billy is going to run the front of the house, and Darryl's hired two servers that he's training at Café Belgie. They will work for Billy, so we need to hire a few more servers as well as some of the kitchen staff. Thankfully, Darryl's pastry chef has agreed to do the desserts for both restaurants." Russ was so excited. The restaurant was really coming together.

"Are you going to be okay this afternoon?" Peter asked as they approached the Acropolis, and Russ knew he was referring to Barry.

"Yes. I think he's gone now. I can almost feel it. Now *I* need to move on." As he said the words, Russ knew what he wanted to do. "Can I see you tonight?" Russ asked. "I have to work dinner at Belgie, but I'd like to see you afterward if that's okay." Now that he'd made up his mind, Russ felt excited and very much at peace with his decision.

"Of course. Call me when you're on your way," Peter said, and Russ leaned down, kissing him lightly before Peter wheeled himself to his car. After watching him go, Russ unlocked the door and went into the restaurant.

Russ got a lot done in the restaurant that afternoon. The tables and chairs were unpacked, and he set them roughly in place so he could see how the dining room would work. He reminded himself to have Billy come over to check it out as well. By the end of the day, the installers were indeed finished, and Russ stood in the middle of what would be his own kitchen. Turning on the burners, he tried everything, checking to make sure it all worked. Every piece of equipment gleamed. It might not have been new, but it looked and felt new, and that was all Russ wanted. He made a note to arrange to get a mop and bring cleaning materials over so he could scrub and sanitize the kitchen. Checking his watch, Russ realized he was going to be late, so he shut things down and turned off the lights. After locking the doors, he walked in the afternoon sunshine toward Café Belgie.

Dinner service was relatively slow, and for that Russ was grateful. He was already tired and he knew Darryl was as well, so at closing time, they cleaned up and Darryl gave him a ride back to the house. During a few lulls while they cleaned, Russ had told Darryl about his altercation with Barry and what he'd done. He wasn't proud of how he'd acted, but Darryl had actually offered him a high five. "I wanted to smack him five seconds after I met him."

"Why didn't I see it? Why didn't anyone tell me?" Russ asked, but he already knew the answer to both questions, and Darryl looked over at him, but didn't answer. Russ knew he hadn't seen it because he hadn't wanted to, and he wouldn't have listened if someone had told him.

"You had to see it for yourself," Darryl finally answered, and Russ knew he was right. "And you did a pretty good job of hiding what was going on." Darryl parked outside the house, and Russ followed him inside after checking that his car was all right. He didn't necessarily need to drive it that often, but he figured Barry might try to damage it or somehow take it back. It was fine, and Russ went inside, where he cleaned up, washing away the scent of kitchen and food.

"Are you going to Peter's?" Darryl asked once he emerged from the bathroom.

"I was. Is that okay?"

"You don't need our permission," Darryl said with a yawn. "I'll lock up after you. Drive safely." Russ got dressed, and as an afterthought, placed a bag with a few clothes in the trunk before riding to Peter's.

It was late, and Peter's house was dark when he pulled up. Thinking maybe he shouldn't have come, Russ actually contemplated leaving so he wouldn't disturb Peter, until he saw one of the lights switch on. Getting out of the car, Russ walked to the front door and knocked before pushing it open.

Peter sat on the sofa, resting under what looked like a thin blanket, watching television. "I didn't mean to keep you up," Russ said as he closed the door behind him.

"You didn't," Peter responded as he sat up. "I was waiting for you. When you asked if you could come over, you sounded so cryptic I was wondering if something was wrong." Russ saw doubt and insecurity in Peter's eyes.

"I didn't mean to worry you," Russ said, walking closer to where Peter sat. Bending down, he placed his hands on Peter's cheeks and kissed him hard and full on his sweet mouth. "That was the last thing I had in mind when I asked if I could come over tonight." Russ knew what he felt, and what Peter wanted—he could see it in Peter's beautiful eyes.

"What changed?" Peter asked. "Something did change, didn't it?"

"Yes," Russ answered resting his forehead on Peter's. "I realized who's been there for me these last few weeks." Russ tilted his head slightly and touched Peter's lips. "I realized I was letting my bastard ex get in the way of someone I want to be with. Someone who makes me happy rather than scared, and someone who touches me as though I'm dear and precious, as opposed to property."

Peter returned Russ's smile. "Should I get off the sofa?"

"That might be a good idea, and if this were a romantic movie, I'd lift you and carry you to the bed myself," Russ quipped. Peter pulled the chair over, sliding into it. Turning off the television, Russ followed Peter to the bedroom. Inside, Russ helped Peter out of his chair and onto the bed. He really wasn't used to being in charge in the bedroom, or anywhere else for that matter, but maybe it was time for him to start. Pulling off his shirt, Russ let it fall to the floor and then toed off his shoes. He saw Peter's eyes widen as he slipped off his pants, letting them join the growing pile on the floor.

"Russ," Peter moaned as he moved toward the bed. "You're amazing."

"No. You are, Peter, and not just on the outside." He helped Peter sit up and then tugged off his shirt before removing Peter's pants. He knew it would be more romantic to disrobe piece by piece, but he was too excited, and this was much easier on Peter, who now lay on the bedding, his underwear tented. "You said last night that you could feel my hands." Russ placed them on Peter's legs. "Can you feel them now?"

"Yes, sort of," Peter answered, and Russ moved them up Peter's olive-toned thighs. "How about now?" he asked, and Peter nodded. Sliding them up further, he slipped his fingers under the leg opening of Peter's briefs, and a soft groan sounded from deep in Peter's throat. "I know you can feel that," Russ said seductively, sliding his fingers beneath the fabric, skimming lightly over the skin at the base of Peter's cock. Peter couldn't move his legs, but Russ could almost swear he could feel him trembling until he realized the entire bed was shaking and it was coming from Peter.

Peter's skin felt hot on his hands, like it was burning him. Russ always expected olive-skinned men to be hairy, but Peter was nearly smooth everywhere, and his soft skin felt wonderful on his hands. "Is this okay?" Russ teased. He could tell by the way Peter's mouth hung open and his breath hitched that his touch was more than okay. Slipping his hand beneath the white cotton, Russ stroked Peter's cock with his fingertips.

"Russ," Peter whined, and Russ pulled his hand away, earning a disappointed groan. Reaching up to Peter's waist, Russ tugged the fabric down Peter's hips and down his legs. He actually whistled softly at the sight of Peter's body. Yes, his legs were thin and weak, but the rest of him was as virile and strong as anyone Russ had ever seen, especially the thick rod pointing straight and proud toward Peter's belly button.

"Damn, you're gorgeous," Russ muttered.

"No, I'm not," Peter argued, and Russ curled his fingers around Peter's cock, watching as his new lover's eyes rolled back and his jaw dropped open.

"Oh yes, you are," Russ whispered. "You look amazing." Russ stroked lightly, and a small moan built. Without letting go, Russ brought their lips together. He expected a deep kiss, but what he got was Peter devouring him. Russ felt fingers card through his hair and then pressure as they sealed their lips together. Peter acted as though he would never let him go, and that was fine with Russ. He didn't want to let go, either. Tightening his grip on Peter's shaft, Russ stroked harder and felt Peter move his hips into the touch. "What do you like?" Russ asked between searing kisses, and Peter shook his head but didn't answer. "You need to help me."

"Nothing you do is wrong, Russ. It can't be, because it's from the heart," Peter told him, locking their eyes briefly before kissing him again.

How long they kissed and touched, Russ had no idea. It seemed to go on forever but last just the blink of an eye. Tilting his head, Russ captured a richly colored nipple between his lips, rolling his tongue around the pebbled bud. Peter called out complete nonsense, and Russ sucked harder, feeling his new lover beginning to go to pieces beneath him. That had never happened to Russ, and as far as he could remember, Barry had never had that effect on him, but damn if it wasn't the sexiest thing on earth. Russ lifted his head away and stared for a few seconds before sucking on the other tight little bud. "Damned if you aren't as sexy as hell."

"Me?" Peter gasped.

"You're damned right, you!" Russ growled as he kissed and sucked a trail across Peter's chest and down his stomach, accompanied by small flutters and gasps. All Peter's noises stopped, and Russ looked up to make sure everything was okay. What he saw was Peter staring wide-eyed, holding his breath. Smiling evilly, Russ pursed his lips and ran them down Peter's cock. As soon as he touched Peter, a high-pitched whine filled the room. Russ moved his head back and forth, sliding his lips up and down the thick shaft before slipping Peter's cock between his lips. He could almost feel the breath whoosh out of Peter's body as Peter's flavor burst onto his tongue.

"Russ. That's so damn good!" Peter sputtered through short panting breaths.

Russ hummed softly around Peter's cock, taking as much as he could. Peter was not a small man, and Russ took all he could before licking the man like a lollipop. With every touch, Peter's noises grew louder and more frantic. Russ knew it wouldn't be long, and he stopped.

"Russ!" Peter groaned.

"It's too soon," Russ soothed, bringing their lips together again. Russ could tell Peter was aching to take charge of things, it was written all over his face, and so was frustration. "Do you have stuff?" Russ asked, and Peter tilted his head toward the table. Russ opened the drawer and saw what looked like a fresh package of condoms.

"Just hoping," Peter explained, and Russ smiled. Opening the package, Russ rolled a condom down Peter's shaft before straddling his lover's body. Popping open the lube, Russ slicked Peter before preparing himself. Getting into position, Russ gripped Peter's shaft and slowly lowered his body.

Peter was big, Russ knew that, but he felt as though he'd gotten larger in the last ten seconds as he entered Russ's body. Closing his eyes and trying to breathe, Russ stopped and waited, letting his body adjust before taking Peter deeper. The lube bottle dropped away, and Russ hadn't even realized he'd still been holding it until he heard it thunk on the floor. He felt Peter's hands on his thighs, stroking and soothing.

Russ sighed loudly when he felt Peter's hips against his butt. "You feel like a furnace," Peter told him.

Russ thought of saying something about beer cans, but then felt Peter move and jolt inside him, and his entire body exploded with tingles of pleasure. "Never felt so full," Russ gasped as he slowly lifted his body up before sliding back down Peter's cock. Damn, the man was a god, and every time he moved, Peter brushed over that spot deep inside. After a few strokes, Russ was seeing stars. As he continued, he forgot his own name and Peter's. Soon they were bouncing on the bed, Peter thrusting into him, and Russ making sounds he didn't think were humanly possible. "Fuck, you're unbelievable," Russ said, but it might have come out as total gibberish, he wasn't really sure, and Peter didn't seem to be faring much better in the coherence department either. The only coherent thought Russ clung to was not to hurt Peter; everything else was a blur.

Russ felt his own cock slapping his belly, and then Peter's fingers circled him, stroking and gripping. The increased ecstasy threatened to overwhelm him, but he rode it out with Peter and he had no intention of stopping. Russ lifted and descended more times than he could count, driving himself onto Peter's shaft, taking him deep. His head throbbed, and every muscle and nerve in his body seemed on hyperdrive.

"I can't last!" Peter cried through gritted teeth.

"Don't. Take me with you," Russ answered through his haze of passion, and he felt Peter tense. With one final drive, Russ impaled himself on Peter and felt the monster cock inside him pulse and throb as Peter cried out his release loud enough for half the town to hear.

Somehow, Russ didn't follow. Instead, he stilled, watching Peter at his most entrancing as he totally went to pieces, soaking in every sensation. Once Peter stilled and caught his breath, Russ felt warm, firm fingers grip him, stroking strongly. Russ couldn't last long, he knew that, but he loved the feel of Peter touching him, so he held out as long as he could before coming in a mind-bending surge of sexual energy. Russ rode out his release and basked in the shared glow with Peter before forcing his legs to work, lifting himself off Peter.

They both gasped when their bodies disconnected, and Russ hurried to the bathroom to get a cloth. After cleaning them, the fastest cleanup in history, Russ rested next to Peter, arms entwined, bodies pressed together. Russ felt happy, truly happy, for the first time in a very long time. Life had taught him not to take it for granted, so he held Peter tight as they drifted to sleep, determined to hold on to what he had for as long as he could.

CHAPTER SEVEN

"OKAY. I know you can't make any promises," Peter said into the Bluetooth connection in his car as he pulled up in front of the Acropolis. "I appreciate your help."

"I have one more idea to try," Peter's lawyer said. "I could keep going, but I don't see any reason to waste your money on a wild goose chase. I'll call you by the end of the week whether I have anything or not, and you can decide where you want to go from there."

"Thank you," Peter said before disconnecting the call. Three weeks ago, he'd engaged an attorney to try to help find his sister, but he was not having much luck. Peter had set a limit on what he was willing to try to spend, and after two weeks, the attorney had found very little. Short of having him traipse all around the western portion of the state looking for the adoption records, there wasn't much else he could do. The attorney had found the birth records in Allegheny County, but the adoption records weren't there. His father couldn't provide any more information, and short of a miracle, Peter was beginning to lose hope. He knew people searched for adoptive siblings and birth parents for years and often came up empty, but he'd really been hoping to find his sister.

Parking the car, Peter got out his chair and rolled up to the front door of the restaurant, pulling it open before gliding inside. "What happened?" Peter gasped as he stared at piles of broken white china everywhere. Russ stood in the center of the floor, looking at him openmouthed.

"I don't know," Russ said barely above a whisper. "The police just left, and they're trying to figure out who could have gotten in here."

"Did they break anything else?" Peter asked, imagining the newly installed kitchen with all its equipment that would be hard to replace. Russ shook his head.

"They broke every dish and glass in the place." Russ gingerly moved toward him, trying not to step on the shards. Peter was still, and as soon as Russ reached him, he was engulfed in a tight hug as Russ practically collapsed onto his lap. "I know it was Barry. He's sending me a message that he can still get to me."

"Has he been following you or calling you?" Peter asked.

"Not that I know of," Russ answered.

"So how do you know it was him?" Peter asked.

Russ continued hugging him and showed no sign of letting go, which was fine with Peter. "Barry bought the house we lived in about three years ago, and when we were moving in, I was helping to unload the truck. I picked up one of the boxes, and as I was carrying it into the house, the bottom fell out of it. The box was full of china, and every single piece of his grandmother's Wedgwood china ended up broken on the sidewalk. He always blamed me for it, said I wasn't carrying the box right."

"So you think he got in here and broke all your dishes? After all this time?" Peter knew he sounded skeptical, and Russ pulled away. "You have to admit, it seems farfetched."

"You don't understand. Barry carries a grudge longer than anyone I've ever met, and I'm sure this was his subtle message. I know it sounds dumb, but this is the type of thing Barry would do. I know it. I couldn't even tell the police because they would have thought me even crazier than you do." The hurt in Russ's voice broke Peter's heart.

"I'm sorry," Peter said, but Russ stepped back, shards of broken glass and pottery cracking under his feet. "Did the police say you could clean this up?" Peter asked, and Russ nodded. "Then get a broom and dustpan. Go outside and around back so you don't damage the floor by walking on the broken glass." Peter hoped that action and doing something to right the wrong would help. Russ stepped around him, and Peter reached for his hand. "I really am sorry, and I believe you." Russ smiled slightly and nodded before leaving through the front door.

Peter pulled out his phone and made a call. "Annette."

"Hey, Peter, what have you got for me?" She sounded cheerful. *Must be one of Jerry's days off.*

"That order we placed for the Acropolis a few weeks ago—I need you to place a duplicate order to replace all their dishes, glasses, and stemware. Someone broke in and smashed everything. We need it ASAP. The restaurant is supposed to open in a few weeks and everything's gone." Peter looked at the destruction around him as he spoke. "Could you let me know when I can tell them to expect delivery?"

"Sure. I'll get the order placed and send you the paperwork they'll need to sign." Peter could already hear Annette typing frantically as they disconnected. Putting his phone away, Peter heard Russ starting to sweep up.

"What did Darryl say?" Peter asked, and Russ stopped sweeping.

"He was livid. When the police got here, they tried to play it off as kids or something, but Darryl pointed out that kids didn't have keys and there was no sign of forced entry." Russ began sweeping again, clearing an initial path. "How he got one, I don't know."

"I've already got my office working on a replacement order," Peter explained, wishing he could help clean up, but his chair would only make things worse.

Peter turned around when the door behind him opened, and Billy walked in with Donnie and Davey right behind, all three of them carrying brooms and dustpans. "Don't use your hands to pick up anything," Billy cautioned.

"Darryl said the one of us who picks up the most gets ice cream," one of the boys told Peter. He wasn't sure which boy was which, but the determined look in his eye told Peter it was going to be that one.

"For helping out, Darryl and I are going to take you *both* for ice cream, and just before school starts we'll take you to Hershey Park. But we need to get this mess all cleaned up. Each of you start in a corner and work toward the middle." Billy pointed, and the boys began sweeping. Once they had a path clear, Peter made his way through to the kitchen. He wanted to check out everything for himself. Nothing looked out of place, but he called the installers and explained what happened, and they agreed to stop by sometime during the day to check out all the lines and equipment.

Rolling back into the dining area, Peter saw Billy and Russ moving tables while the boys swept around them. The sound of broken glass being dumped into trashcans punctuated the sounds of sweeping and talking. "I wasn't expecting you today," Russ said to him as he sat down at a table.

"I was just stopping by to do a final inspection and to see if there was anything more before I had you sign off on everything. You said last night that you'd be here, and a few hours opened up in my day." Peter stayed where he was, and Russ got up and walked to him. "I should have believed you earlier," Peter whispered, and Russ smiled.

"I was upset," Russ told him. Both he and Russ seemed to realize they had an audience at the same time, and after kissing quickly, they broke apart. "Will I see you tonight?"

"I hope so," Peter answered with a relieved grin. "I have things I need to tell you." After saying goodbye to everyone, Peter carefully rolled toward the door, making sure he didn't go over anything that could get in his wheels and eventually cut his hands.

PETER waited up for Russ, dozing in the living room. He'd had a long day, and he'd already napped for a few hours in front of the television in his recliner. He loved when he could get out of his chair and sit like a real person. He knew many people in wheelchairs who spent most of their time in one, but he hated it. Peter transferred himself to his favorite chair or the sofa whenever he could. It made him feel more like he had been before the accident. A car outside caught his attention, and Peter thought he heard someone pull into the driveway. Expecting it to be Russ, he sat up and waited for the familiar knock and the door to open, but it didn't.

Peter listened, but didn't hear any more sounds from outside. Thinking it must have been his imagination, he went back to watching television. After a few minutes, he heard what sounded like someone outside his door, but no one knocked. "Russ, is that you?" Peter called out, but he didn't get an answer. Peter thought he saw movement outside one of his windows, and now he was officially freaked out. Reaching for his phone, he dialed Russ's number, and when he didn't answer, Peter was ready to call the police. Then a car definitely pulled into his driveway, the lights shining into his windows. Closing the phone a few seconds later, he heard Russ's knock, and then the door opened and Russ peered inside. "You okay?"

"Yeah, why?"

Russ stepped inside. "I thought I might have seen someone running away from the far side of the house as I drove up, but I wasn't sure."

"And I thought I saw someone outside the window and was about to call the police." Peter's nervousness increased exponentially. He heard a car pass by the front of the house and Russ peered out the windows.

"There's nothing there now," Russ said as he let the curtains fall back into place. "We could call the police anyway," Russ suggested, but Peter shook his head.

"It's probably our imaginations. After what happened, it's probably natural." Peter settled back in the chair, turning off the television, and Russ sat down as well. "I heard from the lawyer, but he hasn't been able to find much." He wanted to change the subject so maybe the weird feeling in his stomach would go away.

"Is that what you wanted to tell me earlier?" Russ asked,

"Yeah. He's not very hopeful. I could probably find out more if I threw a lot of money at it, but I don't have the funds, and there's no guarantee of success if I did."

"Are you giving up?" Russ stood up and settled on the arm of Peter's chair.

"No. He has one more thing to try. I'm not giving up, but I can't afford to spend thousands, either. I've contacted some adoption search agencies, and they might have some ideas too." Peter was trying to put the best face on it, knowing there wasn't really much hope, but he felt he couldn't give up completely. His sister was out there, somewhere.

"Is there anything I can do to help?" Russ asked, leaning closer, and Peter felt some of the warmth from Russ's body.

"I don't think so," Peter said and looked into Russ's eyes with a half smile. "Unless you have talents you haven't told me about."

Russ smiled a sexy, slightly crooked grin. "Oh, I have talents." Peter shivered as Russ skimmed his hands up Peter's arm, just shy of tickling, but enough to raise goose bumps on his skin and send a shiver down his spine. Russ's lightly touched his chin, and then Russ leaned close, kissing him softly. "Why don't we go to bed?"

Peter nodded and reached to pull his chair close. It took him a few minutes, but he transferred himself to the chair and followed Russ down the hallway. In the bedroom, Peter started to move to the bed, but Russ stopped him with a light touch before leaning down to kiss him again, this time deeper.

Russ stopped kissing long enough to pull off Peter's shirt, and then he was kissed again. Peter wondered just what Russ had in mind, but those thoughts didn't last long as his body reacted to Russ's touch on his skin and the kisses on his lips. When he felt Russ kiss down his chest, Peter held his breath, tilting his head backward and moving his hips forward. Russ continued slowly kissing a passage down his body, stopping to suck, swirling his tongue around each nipple before continuing on.

Russ opened Peter's pants, sliding his zipper down, and his breath caught with delicious anticipation. He hoped to God Russ was going to do what he thought he was gonna do.

His underwear was pulled lower, and Peter snapped his head forward as Russ's encircled his shaft with strong fingers. Peter's breath came in shallow pants as Russ stroked with agonizing slowness up and down his length. Peter forced his eyes to stay open and saw the most amazing expression of Russ's face, a touch of awe mixed with unabashed lustful passion. "We should move to the bed," Peter gasped.

"Not yet," Russ told him before lowering his lips over Peter's cock.

The air whooshed from Peter's lungs, and he cried out softly as his cock was surrounded by wet heat. Peter's eyes drifted closed, and he carded his fingers through Russ's hair. In his chair, he couldn't move his hips, and the complete lack of control was frustratingly erotic. "Oh God, Russ, suck me!" And Russ did. Peter was taken to the root, and he felt one of Russ's hands slide around his hip and into his pants to cup one of his cheeks. Russ took him deep, and Peter mumbled a deep, throaty groan as he felt Russ's nose against his skin. Peter felt on top of the world, and then Russ skimmed a finger over his opening. Peter lay back, head lolling over the back of the chair as Russ drove him higher and higher.

Peter wondered for a few seconds how Russ could breathe, then Russ backed away only to take him deep again, this time with the tip of his finger entering Peter's body. He cried out in surprise as Russ sucked him deep once again, pushing his finger slightly further into his body. His mind was overloading, and Peter almost begged Russ to stop, but then Russ touched him inside and Peter forgot everything in the world except Russ. Nothing else mattered except what his lover was doing right here and now.

He wanted to thrust but couldn't, and Russ seemed to sense that, because he bobbed his head, fucking his own mouth on Peter's cock, and the sensations that went through him had Peter shaking. "Russ!" Peter cried before swallowing hard, his chest heaving to catch a breath. Then Russ stopped, holding the head of Peter's clock in his mouth, swirling his tongue around the sensitive head. Peter had never felt anything like it, and he gripped the armrests of the chair to steady himself.

Russ began moving his head again, sucking him hard and deep. Peter didn't know what to do, so he gave up any pretense of control and gave himself completely over to Russ. As soon as he did, he felt Russ press his finger fully inside, and Russ sucked harder than he ever had. Almost immediately, Peter felt his body tighten as a tingling began in his balls. He tried to hold out, to make the sensation last every second he could, but he was soon overwhelmed. His arms began to shake, and he clamped his eyes closed as his orgasm built. He almost felt dizzy as Russ continued his ministrations. Russ touched that spot inside him once again, and Peter lost the last of his control. Crying out nonsense, he came down Russ's throat, feeling his lover swallowing around him.

It took him a while to come back to himself, but when he did, he saw Russ smiling back at him. Then Russ kissed him, and Peter tasted himself on Russ's tongue. Peter held onto the arms of the chair, feeling as though he were about to slide out. It had been a very long time since he'd felt anything so heady. His body was so relaxed and his mind still swirled so much he didn't trust his own senses.

"Now we can move you to the bed," Russ said, and Peter nodded. Russ moved him closer, carefully guiding him onto the mattress. He expected Russ to get undressed and join him, but instead, he removed all of Peter's clothes before lightly stroking Peter's back. "Are you okay?"

"More than okay," Peter said, reaching under Russ's shirt. "Are you leaving?"

Russ shook his head and pulled off his shirt. Peter stroked the exposed skin, and Russ stilled. Then he slid off the bed, removing the rest of his clothes before climbing in next to Peter, hugging him close. Peter rolled over, and Russ spooned to his back, a thick, hard column of flesh pressing to Peter's butt. "Is that what you want?" Peter asked, a little concerned.

"Only if you do," Russ answered in his ear, lips sucking on his lobe.

"Yeah, but I really don't know how it will work," Peter answered, and he felt Russ slide his hand down his side. Russ trailed his lips behind, and Peter quickly forgot about things like logistics as Russ touched and kissed him. Reaching to the bedside table, Peter found the lube and a condom, handing both to Russ behind him.

Russ took the supplies, and Peter heard a snick. Then a slick finger pressed into him, followed quickly by another. "I want to be inside you," Russ told him softly, and Peter nodded. Russ once more touched the spot inside, and Peter closed his eyes, moaning softly. He'd always been sensitive, but he didn't remember ever responding like he was with Russ. Russ slipped his fingers out of him, and Peter groaned as an emptiness settled around him.

Peter heard the package opening and imagined what Russ would look like as he rolled the condom down his cock. Russ settled his arms around his chest, and Peter felt Russ slowly press inside him. "Breathe, sweetheart, and try to relax."

Peter did both and concentrated on relaxing his muscles, taking Russ inside his body. "So full."

"I know. That's how you make me feel," Russ told him as he slid deeper, and Peter nodded slowly. Russ continued kissing his shoulder and back, and Peter breathed deeply as he felt Russ's hips against his butt. Russ stilled, and Peter continued his measured breathing, letting the unfamiliar sensations subside. The pain had gone, thankfully. Then Russ began to move, very slowly at first, and pleasure replaced the pain like a wave gently sliding into a footprint on the sand. Peter almost didn't realize it until he once again began to moan. He'd just come a few minutes earlier, but he was already hard again.

Russ reached over him, wrapping a hand around his dick, stroking slowly. Peter wasn't sure he had the energy to come again, but his body had other ideas, and as Russ thrust into him, his skin tingled. Everywhere Russ touched, Peter could feel goose bumps rising. "You're beautiful like this," Russ said from behind him.

"How can you tell?" Peter gasped.

"I can see you in the mirror. Your eyes closed, skin flushed. It's such a turn-on to know I'm doing this." Russ drove deep and held still. "You weren't like this before, were you?"

It took Peter a second to realize what Russ was asking, but then he nodded, and Russ withdrew, nearly pulling out before driving back into him with enough power to rock the bed. "Love you, Russ," Peter cried as Russ's cock dragged across the magic spot. Russ held him through the quivers that followed and then did it again. How many times Russ made him shake, he didn't know, but he felt Russ's rhythm begin to falter, and Peter knew his lover's release was extremely close.

Russ stopped moving and said nothing, like he was listening. Then, slowly, he began thrusting again, whispering soft words into Peter's ear. "Fuck me, Russ," Peter began chanting under his breath, moving to meet his lover's movements as best he could.

Russ was a sex machine; that was the only way Peter could describe it. For God knows how much time, Russ kept him teetering on the edge, stopping with agonizing patience whenever he felt Peter was close to the edge, backing them off before driving them even higher. Peter's mind threatened to melt as Russ held him, sweat running down both their bodies. Peter could feel it every time Russ touched him. "Russ, please. I can't take much more," Peter begged as once again Russ pushed his hand away from his cock, replacing it with his own, but never quite giving Peter exactly what he needed to come.

Russ's tightened his grip on his dick and Peter felt the excitement rising once again. He wasn't sure if this was it, but he was more than ready. Closing his eyes, Peter felt the pressure build and build. It had been so close to the surface so many times his own body seemed to doubt itself, but then Russ tightened his grip, stroking harder and faster. Peter groaned and moaned, panting quickly as his release became imminent.

Peter heard Russ groan in his ear, driving into his body and then stilling, Russ's large cock pulsing and throbbing inside Peter's body. Tightening his muscles around Russ, he heard him cry out something unintelligible, but Peter had no time to dwell on it because he was coming himself. Peter heard, "I love you too," as wave after wave of pleasure, each one higher than the previous, broke over him and threatened to carry him away.

Peter stilled with Russ inside him, his hand resting on his cock. Slowly, his mind checked to make sure everything was okay. After an experience that intense, Peter almost expected some sort of pain, but there wasn't, just the sweetest afterglow of his life. Then he remembered—he'd told Russ how he felt.

Russ still held him, and Peter groaned slightly as Russ pulled out from inside him. Then Russ rolled away, and the arms that had held him slipped away. He felt Russ get off the bed, and Peter closed his eyes, feeling quite alone all of a sudden. He knew Russ was just in the bathroom, Peter could hear the water running, but he still seemed so far away. He'd bared his heart to Russ, and Peter thought he remembered Russ saying he loved him, but he couldn't be sure. Yes, he knew how he felt, and he'd told Russ the truth, even in the height of passion, but he couldn't be sure if that was just the sex speaking for Russ or not.

Russ returned, leaning over the bed. "Lie back." Peter turned onto his back and felt the warm cloth on his skin. "I hate to say this, but we made a bit of a mess."

Peter looked around and laughed at the giant wet spot on the sheet. "I guess so."

Russ took the cloth and walked back toward the bathroom, Peter watching his tight butt sway. After taking care of things in the bathroom, Russ left the bedroom, and Peter wondered what was going on until he heard doors opening and closing. Russ then returned with fresh sheets. Russ brought the chair close to the bed, and Peter transferred himself to it. Russ stripped the bed and remade it before helping Peter back onto the mattress. "You can put the sheets in the basket in the corner," Peter said as he settled in bed.

Russ turned out the lights, and Peter felt him get into bed, moving to curl right behind him. He wanted to ask if Russ meant what he said, but he didn't. He was afraid. If Russ said it had just been the passion, he'd be heartbroken, so he kept quiet, resting in Russ's arms, feeling light kisses on his shoulder.

CHAPTER EIGHT

RUSS hated to get up, but he had to get in to work and then check on the Acropolis. They'd gotten everything cleaned up and had the locks changed. Billy had made him swear he wouldn't go anyplace alone, and Darryl had started working to get an alarm system for the building. They had hoped it wouldn't be necessary, but Darryl was insisting. Peter had mumbled softly when Russ had gotten out of bed and had barely woken at all when he'd kissed him goodbye.

Russ knew he was falling in love; that was becoming quite clear to him. But he couldn't be sure if he was on the rebound or not. When they had been making love, Russ had told Peter how he'd felt, and he didn't regret it. He hadn't lied—he did love Peter. He just wished he knew what was happening with him. Billy would tell him to go with his heart, and Billy would be right. Russ just wished he knew what that meant.

Driving to Darryl and Billy's, he let himself in and went upstairs to his room. They had already left for work, and after a quick shower, he headed back out, calling Darryl on the way. "Where do you need me this morning?" he asked when Darryl answered.

"We're all set here. Go on to the Acropolis and get everything you can set up so that once the replacement dishes arrive, we can start training the waitstaff. Billy has set up interviews for additional staff for tomorrow morning at the new location, so we want the place looking as good as we can get it."

"Will do," Russ agreed.

"And call me when you get there to let me know everything is okay, or Billy will kill both of us." Darryl's voice held a hint of amusement regarding his mother hen of a husband.

"I will," Russ promised as he made the final turn. Hanging up, Russ parked and looked at the dark building. The sun was just beginning to come up, and Russ wished he'd asked to have someone else come over so he wouldn't be alone. Shutting off the engine, Russ got out of the car and hurried to the back door, unlocking it before scurrying inside, shutting and locking it behind him.

Russ listened in the empty building and heard no movement. Reaching for the lights, he flipped every switch, lighting up the entire kitchen. Walking through, he turned on all the dining room lights, checking to make sure everything was okay and that he was alone. Only after he'd checked everything did Russ begin to relax.

Russ began work by sweeping the floors again to make sure everything was truly cleaned up. Then he began resetting the tables and chairs.

"You got my message."

Russ whipped around and saw Barry standing inside the front door, closing it behind him. "What are you doing here? How did you get in?"

"Like I said, you got my message." Barry locked the door, and Russ saw him charge over to where he was working. "You think you can get away from me?" Barry grabbed his wrists, and Russ struggled. "I love you, goddamn it, and you're going to listen to me."

"Barry, let go of me!" Russ lashed out with his foot, connecting hard with Barry's shin. Barry cried out and let go of his wrists, and Russ backed away, putting a couple tables between them. "What is wrong with you?" Russ screamed. He knew he probably should try to keep Barry calm, but he was way beyond that. "I'm not your property, and you can't make me do what I don't want to."

"You wanna bet?" Barry took a step closer, and Russ picked up a chair to use as a weapon. "I heard you last night at the cripple's house. And it would be a shame if anything were to happen to him. People in wheelchairs get hurt all the time. You see it on the news."

The chair he'd been holding hit the floor, and Russ felt as though Barry had punched him in the stomach. "Th… that was you," Russ muttered, staring at Barry as he tried to keep as much distance between them as possible. "What are you doing, Barry? Hiding in bushes and following me, peering in windows, threatening to hurt people? What's happened to you?" The last of the feelings he had for Barry fell away, and Russ saw him clearly, probably for the first time in his life. Peter, Billy, Darryl, they'd all helped him, and over time he'd come to realize that Barry had been controlling and abusive, but he hadn't considered that Barry might have gone around the bend. But he certainly seemed to have done just that. His eyes had an almost feral look that Russ hadn't seen before.

"Nothing. You left. I'm perfectly fine!" Barry's answers made little sense at all.

"You are not! You were controlling, but you weren't always mean. We had some good times together, but it's over now." Russ kept his voice as calm as he could. He wanted to call for help, but something told him it would make Barry even more frantic, and he wasn't sure what Barry would do. "You need to move on and get some help."

"No, I don't. What I need is for you to come home," Barry said firmly, but Russ thought he heard a touch of pleading beneath the words. He obviously had a one-track mind, and he wasn't getting off it. Russ's phone began ringing in his pocket, and he grabbed for it, answering it as fast as he could. "Barry is here and I need help," Russ said without waiting to see who it was. Barry lunged for him, and Russ dropped the phone as he tried to get away. Barry kicked it across the floor, and it hit the baseboard, breaking into multiple pieces. "I love you, Russ, and I need you."

Russ kept backing away, trying to figure out how he could get out of the building and to his car. He had no idea what Barry would do to him if he caught him, and he didn't want to find out. Barry's eyes were wide, and he looked frantically around the room every few seconds. "I love you too, Barry, and I probably always will, but we aren't a couple anymore, and you need to realize that." The words sounded so reasonable in Russ's ears, even if they mostly rang hollow. "Things have changed and we can't go back. You need to move on."

"No!" Barry lunged for him, knocking over one of the tables, and it hit the floor with a bang. Russ jumped back, remaining just out of Barry's reach. God, he hoped whoever had called got here soon or sent someone. He was fast running out of options. Barry had maneuvered him away from the kitchen door, and he realized he was being herded toward one of the corners and then there would be no place to go. Russ's heart pounded as he tried to keep his head and think, but he could already feel a sense of panic rising from inside him that he had to work to keep tamped down.

Pounding on the back door drew Barry's attention. "Russ, are you inside?"

"Yes," he yelled at the top of his lungs. "Barry is here too." He could hear the panic in his own voice. "The front door is unlocked!" Russ didn't know that for sure, but Barry turned to look and Russ ran for the kitchen. He could hear Barry behind him, but his mind was focused on unlocking the back door. He reached it and pulled it open as he felt Barry's hand on his arm.

Billy and Darryl raced inside, with Peter right behind, and Barry lugged him toward the kitchen door. Russ lashed out at him and managed to pull away. By the time Russ turned around, Barry was already out of the kitchen, and a few seconds later he heard the front door bang closed.

Russ stared at the three of them, and no one moved until he stumbled. Then Russ was being helped up by Darryl while Billy raced to get a chair. "Are you okay?" Peter asked as Darryl lowered Russ into a chair. Russ felt his hand in Peter's and pulled it away.

"He saw us last night. He was in the bushes, and he said he saw us and heard us." Russ felt tears push to the surface, and he tried to hold them back. "He was outside your house, and he threatened you." Russ pulled his arms in, his body trying to curl into a ball.

"I took care of Barry once, and I'll do it again," Peter said, and Russ felt him take his hand one more time.

Russ tried to pull away, but Peter held his hand tight. "He'll hurt you because of me. He was outside your house and he heard us." Russ could barely form the words. He kept trying to breathe, but he couldn't seem to get enough air. "He said people in wheelchairs get hurt all the time." Russ closed his eyes and images of Peter rolling down his basement stairs or falling sideways off his front porch flashed in front of his eyes. Russ felt his head begin to spin.

"I'll be fine," Peter said, and Russ shook his head, which only made the spinning worse. "Breathe slow and steady," Peter told him, and Russ did as he was told, the spinning beginning to go away. "You're going to be fine, and no one is going to hurt either of us."

"How can you be sure?" Russ asked, afraid to open his eyes, but he did it anyway. The room moved for a few seconds and then settled down.

"The police are on their way," Darryl interrupted, and Russ looked up at him, feeling a whole new level of fear. "They're going to help," Darryl added as he patted Russ's shoulder.

Peter still held his hand, and Russ tried once again to pull it away, but Peter held on, leaning close to him. "If you try to do something as noble as pull away from me for my own protection, I'll tickle you until you can't see straight."

Russ looked into Peter's eyes and saw that he was serious, but with a touch of mischief that intensified when Peter actually ran his hand along Russ's ribs. "Come on," he whined as he squirmed to get away.

"Don't say I didn't warn you," Peter told him, and Russ let go of some of the fear, leaving his hand where it was. Russ lowered his eyes and stared at his feet without seeing them, trying not to think about what Barry had said, but the more he tried, the more he felt the words writing themselves on his soul. "This is not your fault," Peter whispered into his ear.

"I know that," he answered quickly, probably too quickly, because he saw Peter's expression darken.

"Do you? Because it isn't your fault. This is Barry's fault. You had nothing to do with him sneaking around my house, and you had nothing to do with him coming here today. He did all that on his own," Peter told him, and Russ tried to listen. He really did, but the words seemed to bounce off his ears. "Hey!" He felt Peter's fingers on his chin. "I'm serious. This isn't your fault at all."

"Okay," Russ agreed automatically. "But what if he does something to you because of me? That will be my fault because I could have stopped it."

"No, you can't, sir," a strange, firm voice said from in front of him, and Russ saw a shiny pair of black shoes enter his field of vision. Lifting his eyes, Russ looked into the surprisingly soft eyes of a police officer. "What someone else does is their responsibility, not yours." Russ watched blankly as he pulled up one of the chairs and sat in front of him. "I'm officer Aaron Giles." Russ stared at the extended hand before reaching out to shake it. "Why don't you tell me what happened."

Russ opened his mouth to say that he would rather not, and before he knew it everything came tumbling out. The way Barry had followed him, the abuse before he'd left, his suspicions that Barry had been behind the break-in and destruction of the dishes. He kept talking until his throat hurt. He told the officer how Barry had treated him and what he would do to him both in and out of bed. He kept expecting the police officer to look away in disgust, but his eyes never wavered and his expression remained compassionate.

"Do you want to press charges?" the police officer asked once Russ was done talking, and Russ shook his head.

"I just want him to leave me alone," Russ said weakly, and he realized that he was still holding Peter's hand. "To leave us alone," Russ amended, and he looked at Peter, who nodded and smiled back at him.

"I think we can help with that," Officer Giles said. "I'd like you to apply for a protection from abuse order. It's like a restraining order, but more powerful."

"Don't you have to be married?" Russ asked blankly.

"No. It's for any form of domestic abuse," Officer Giles explained. "You meet all the requirements, and we can help you get one. I'll put it into my report, and we can forward it to the court. They're very cooperative in cases like yours. Once we get the order prepared, all we need is for a judge to sign it, and that shouldn't be too hard to get. Once that happens, I'll serve it to this Barry Spencer myself and put the fear of God into him at the same time. Is that what you want?" Russ nodded, and the police officer stood up. Russ watched him walk to where Darryl stood.

"Russ may not want to press charges, but if you can prove Barry broke in here yesterday, I will for the destruction of property." Darryl sounded angry, and Russ turned away, hoping it wasn't because of him. Russ blocked out the rest of the conversation and turned his attention to Peter.

"I'm sorry you got dragged into all this." Russ sighed and closed his eyes, wishing everything would just go away.

The officer returned to Russ. "I'm going to head back to the station. I have your statement for the abuse order, and I'd like you to come in this afternoon to look it over and sign it. We'll then pass it on to your lawyer," the officer said. "None of this is your fault." Russ nodded blankly and watched as the uniformed officer walked out the back door.

"He's right, you know," Peter said once the officer was gone. "You didn't do any of this."

"I know." Russ turned to Peter. "But if he did anything to you...."

"That's what he wants you to think."

"It's working," Russ quipped, but he couldn't hold back a smile. "God, I'm a mess."

"We're all going back to the restaurant. Everything here will keep till tomorrow, and Billy will help you get everything set up for the interviews in the morning," Darryl pronounced as he locked the front door and herded everyone out toward the back. "One of us will come over tonight to make sure everything is okay."

Russ followed the others, looking back inside the kitchen. When Darryl first told him he was going to be the chef at his own restaurant, Russ remembered he'd been so excited. Now, after the last month or so, he wasn't sure he wanted to do it anymore. Barry was turning his dream into a nightmare.

"Did you say something?" Peter asked from next to him, and Russ shook his head.

Russ closed the kitchen door and made sure it was locked. "Barry's not going to take this away from me," he vowed quietly before following Peter to his car while the others left, but not before making Russ promise to come right there.

"You really had me scared when I called this morning," Peter told him as he shifted into the car. "When I heard what you said, I called Darryl right away. I probably should have called the police. I didn't think; I just reacted."

"You did good, thank you." Russ felt his mind clearing from all the stress and near panic. "I had no idea what to do, and I couldn't take my eyes off Barry long enough to actually do anything." He'd felt nearly helpless.

"You kept him away from you long enough for help to arrive." Peter reached out and took Russ's hand. "If anything would have happened to you, I'd have killed Barry myself." The fierceness in Peter's eyes left little doubt that he would definitely try. "Barry can say what he wants and try to do what he wants, but I'll be damned if he's going to hurt either of us. None of this is your fault."

"You already said that," Russ commented as he closed Peter's door, and the driver's side window slid down.

"And I'll keep saying it until you believe it." Peter motioned him closer, and Russ leaned into the open window for a kiss. "How late do you work tonight?"

"I don't know. I was supposed to work here, so I'll probably do paperwork and stuff at Café Belgie before helping Darryl. Will you stop by after you're done with your calls?"

"You better believe it, and I'll check on the dish order as well." Peter kissed him again, and then Russ stepped back. As Peter pulled out of the small parking lot, Russ mouthed, "I love you," lifting his hand to wave. He remembered telling Peter the night before, and he'd heard Peter say the same to him, but neither of them had talked about it afterward, and he wasn't sure if it was just the sex talking for Peter.

Looking around, Russ hurried to his car and climbed in, locking the doors before starting the engine.

RUSS worked hard, keeping his mind off Barry. At lunchtime, Robert came in and handed him a piece of paper. "What's this?" Russ asked as he took it.

"This is the documentation you need for the protection from abuse order. Sign it and have it witnessed, and I'll walk it over to family court this afternoon. Normally there would be a hearing, but I saw his abuse firsthand, as did many others," Robert explained as Russ found a pen. "I spoke with Officer Giles this morning. Once the order is in place, he will serve it himself after work."

Russ signed the paper, and Billy witnessed his signature. "Why is everyone doing this for me?" Russ asked once it was done. "Even Officer Giles, who doesn't know me from Adam, was so nice."

"You have friends, Russ, and as for Office Giles, you'll have to ask him." Robert took the paper and put it in his case before walking back through the kitchen to the dining room.

"Can it be this easy?" Russ asked Darryl, who smiled but didn't answer. Russ was beginning to hope that it actually could as he took his place next to Darryl. They worked the lunch service and then ate with the staff once the restaurant closed for the afternoon.

A knock on the front door as they finished caught everyone's attention, and Russ hurried to let Peter inside. "I finished early and thought I would see how you're doing," Peter said as he rolled inside.

"I'm pretty good. Robert is helping me get the order to keep Barry away, and the officer is going to deliver it, so hopefully now Barry will get the message. And you're here, so my day is definitely looking up." Russ stopped at the curious look on Peter's face. "What is it?"

"I guess we both got good news. I decided to race, and I'm going to the regional wheelchair races next month. Will you be able to go with me?"

Russ whooped, and then colored as everyone in the restaurant looked at him. "I'll try. When is it?"

"Sunday, September 10," Peter said, and Russ nodded because the restaurants would be closed. "I was afraid they would be held on Saturday and you wouldn't be able to come," Peter explained, but Russ cut him off with a kiss. "I take it you're happy."

"I'm happy you're excited about racing. When you told me you used to run, I knew it wasn't the same, but I hoped you'd get something out of it."

Peter scoffed lightly. "You've been cheering me on at every practice for the last few weeks. Yeah, I like it, and I'm especially pleased you found the club for me." Peter pulled him down into another kiss, and the rest of the peanut gallery still sitting at the table whooped and hollered until Peter released him from the soul-touching kiss. Russ colored but did his best to ignore them as he and Peter moved toward the table.

Everyone gave him and Peter a hard time for a few minutes until the conversation moved on. "Have you had any luck finding your sister?" Billy asked during a lull in the conversation.

"Not really, and it looks like I'm going to need to give up for now. We found the birth records, but not the adoption records. My attorney told me it would take some luck, and we really didn't have any." Peter's phone rang, and he pushed away from the table before answering it. Russ watched as the smile slipped off Peter's face, replaced by worry and concern. All Peter said were what sounded like answers to questions. "Can you give me a day to think about it?" Peter listened for a few minutes more before saying goodbye and hanging up.

Peter slowly rolled back to the table, and Russ saw the confused, concerned look on his face. "Is it your dad?" Russ asked, not sure what else could get Peter this upset. Quite frankly, the look on his face was scaring Russ just a little.

"No, Dad's fine," Peter answered blankly, but he didn't say anything more, and while Russ was curious, he didn't press. Since lunch was nearly over, the others finished eating and then began clearing away the dishes, but Russ had lost his appetite, not that he'd had much of one to begin with. He took his plate to the dishroom, returning to find that Peter hadn't moved and was staring at the tablecloth.

"Do you want to talk about it?" Russ asked as he sat back down.

"It's nothing bad, just a bit surprising, I guess." Peter looked up. "After my accident, there were a few times when it wasn't completely clear that I was going to live. My parents added me to a database of possible organ donors, which was fine. That was a call from the hospital in Hershey. They have a person in Florida who needs a bone marrow transplant, and I might be a possible match. They asked if I was still willing to come in so they can do some tests to see if I'm a match. Their records show a high probability, but they need to be sure."

"Are you going to do it?" Russ asked, taking Peter's hand. "Is there any risk to you?"

"I don't know," Peter answered, barely above a whisper. "I think I should try. When I was in the hospital, I needed blood, and I got some because someone else donated it. Without that I would have died." Peter turned toward him, and Russ leaned forward, touching his forehead to Peter's.

"I know what I said to you last night and I meant it." Russ swallowed. "Since I met you, I've been drawn to you, and in a short time I've developed feelings for you that have come as a bit of a surprise." Peter pulled away, looking dubious. "Falling in love with you wasn't a surprise, just how fast it happened, and I think I know why. You're one of the most giving people I've ever met. You've been there for me through this whole thing with Barry when most guys would have run for the hills. I wouldn't have blamed you if you had, but you didn't."

"So you think I should do this," Peter whispered.

Russ shook his head. "I'm saying I'll be there if you decide to do this." Russ wrapped his arms around Peter's neck. "I love you, Peter, and I'll stick with you the whole way, just like you did for me, whatever you decide to do." Russ tilted his head, and Peter kissed him.

"You really love me?" Peter asked, and Russ nodded with a smile.

"How could anyone not love you?" Russ asked, and he saw his smile returned, bright and warm.

"You know, it's hard loving someone who can't walk," Peter told him as his smile faded slightly.

"No." Russ shook his head. "Loving you is easy." As soon as he said the words, he realized that loving Peter was probably the most natural thing he'd ever done in his life. It felt right.

"There are things I'll never be able to do with you," Peter said with a swallow, and Russ shrugged. "Are you sure?"

"Yes."

Peter smiled an eye-crinkling, cheek-dimpling grin. "I love you too."

"I hate to break up you two lovebirds," Billy said from the far end of the table, "but I have to get ready for dinner."

"I should help Darryl," Russ said, but he made no move to stand up yet as he looked into Peter's eyes, basking in their warmth.

"I should go make some calls," Peter said without moving.

"I should throw water on both of you," Billy told them as he pulled the tablecloth off the table in front of them. They both chuckled, and Russ got up to go to the kitchen while Peter headed for the front door.

"I'll call you later," Peter said before leaving the restaurant. Russ waved at him through the windows before going back to work.

The afternoon and early evening were quiet and without drama. Peter called to tell him that the dishes were on their way and should be delivered early the following week. Robert also called to tell him that the order had been signed and that Barry was being served that evening. "If he tries to bother you again, call the police, let them know there is an order, and he'll be immediately arrested." Russ thanked Robert and went back to work with a smile on his face. He knew it wasn't ironclad, but Barry had to get the message now, and he had backup. As he prepared the veal for that evening's special, he wondered why he'd waited so long. He kept expecting an angry phone call from Barry all evening, but nothing came. "Go on home,"

Darryl said as the dinner rush began to wind down. "We've got things here, and you have a full day tomorrow. Billy's leaving as well, so he'll follow you home, just in case."

"Thanks, Darryl," Russ said as he finished what he was doing. Russ cleaned up his station and changed before finding Billy in the dining room. They left the restaurant through the back door together, and true to Darryl's word, Billy followed him home. Everything seemed to be going well. Barry had been told to stay away from him, and Peter loved him. He was tempted to call Peter and see if he could go over, but he decided he needed to think and let everything that had happened sink in. He was happy, but Russ knew that when he was happy was the time when things usually changed, and not necessarily for the better. As he parked his car, Russ hoped that wouldn't happen this time.

CHAPTER NINE

PETER woke in a hospital bed, looking up at the ceiling. "Are you in much pain?" a warm female voice asked, and Peter gently rocked his head. He was surprised, but there was no pain—there wasn't much of anything at all—and he closed his eyes again. The second time he opened them, there was pain, a lot of it. The nurse asked him, and this time he whimpered. She kept pressing him for some sort of number, and he managed to squeak out a word. She must have understood, because a few minutes later the pain subsided. They had said he shouldn't experience too much discomfort. That had been a crock of shit.

He felt someone take his hand, and Peter rolled his head on the pillow to see Russ standing next to him. Russ didn't ask questions; he simply smiled and held his hand. "The doctor said everything went well," Russ told him. "He said you'd be in some pain for a while, but it shouldn't last too long."

"I hope not," Peter answered and closed his eyes, holding onto Russ's hand tightly. "Where's Dad?"

"He'll be right back," Russ told him, and Peter nodded. It had been surprising to him how fast things had happened. The day after the call from the hospital, he'd agreed to the tests, and they'd asked if he could come in right away. Once the tests had been done, they had made room in the schedule for the surgery to take some of the marrow cells from his hip. "The doctor said the results were really good. They got what they needed, and the tissue is already on its way to Florida. He even said that by the time we go to bed, the recipient should have received the transplant."

"That's nice," Peter said, his mind floating on the painkillers. "I hope everything works out."

"It will," Russ said, squeezing his hand. Peter stopped fighting the urge to sleep and let it go.

Movement woke him and Peter opened his eyes, shutting them right away again as the ceiling moved above him. "They're moving you to a room, and if you're up to it, you can go home tomorrow," Peter heard his father's accented voice tell him. Turning his head, he saw Russ walking alongside him. The pain was already lessening, and once he reached the hospital room, a nurse was there to check him over. "If you call 7200, the kitchen will arrange some dinner for you."

Peter heard Russ pick up the phone, but he didn't pay attention. Peter dozed on and off. Once, when he woke up, Russ tried to feed him what had to be the worst food on earth. After choking down a few bites—how they managed to mess up mashed potatoes was beyond him—he closed his eyes and fell asleep. He woke to a dark room, and when he looked over, he saw Russ sleeping in the chair next to the bed. Peter smiled and looked around, feeling wide awake. He thought about turning on the television, but hospitals had rules about crap like that, so he closed his eyes once again and fell back to sleep.

"Are you feeling better?" a soft, deep voice asked, and Peter felt strong hands touching his arm.

"Yes. The pain is much better."

"Most of what you're feeling now is the residual from the anesthetic, and that should finish wearing off soon. Can you lift your legs?" the nurse asked.

"No," he answered, figuring he could have some fun.

"Could you try?"

"No." Peter smiled at the nurse and decided to take pity on him. "If you check my chart closer, you'll see I couldn't when I came in here." Peter motioned toward his chair. "That's not one of yours."

"Sorry," the nurse said, but Peter just waved his hand. "I was just having some fun with you."

"You must be feeling better, then," the nurse commented as he placed Peter's arm in a blood pressure cuff and started the machine. Peter heard Russ stirring and turned to look at him while the nurse continued checking things out. Once he was done, he pushed back the curtain and left the room. Breakfast arrived a while later, and Peter stared at it before eating the fruit and some of the cereal. The rest looked gross.

"Are you going to get something to eat?" Peter asked Russ.

"Actually, your dad said he'd be back this morning and that he'd bring food."

"Thank God," Peter said, pushing back the tray. "Everyone says hospital food has gotten better, but this stuff is terrible. What I really want is a cup of coffee." Russ humored him and moved the breakfast tray out of the way. "Have they said when I can go home?"

"All they told me yesterday was today or tomorrow," Russ said as he moved closer to the bed. "I'm glad you're feeling better." Russ looked out toward the hallway and then moved close for a kiss, which made Peter feel a whole lot better.

The sound of a throat clearing broke them apart, and Peter looked toward the door to see his dad shifting uncomfortably from foot to foot, carrying a bag. Once Russ moved away, his father began unpacking food. Russ moved the remnants of the hospital breakfast to the top of the dresser, and Peter's dad used the mobile bed tray to set out the goodies he'd brought, and those goodies included three cups of the most aromatic coffee Peter had ever smelled in his life. Then a Styrofoam container came out of the bag. When Peter's dad opened it, the hospital room filled with the scent of his father's cinnamon buns. "Dad, you're going to have half the hospital in here," Peter scolded as he reached for one of the delectable rolls, breaking off a piece and popping it into his mouth. "I feel even better already."

"It always worked when you were young," his dad said, and Peter nodded and continued eating as Russ took a bun as well.

"What's all this?" the doctor asked as he walked into the room, and Peter looked up at him, guiltily licking his fingers. Peter saw him look at the tray on the dresser and then back at Peter, not saying a word. "The nurse said your pain level's down, and you're obviously feeling better."

"Do you know anything about the recipient?" Peter asked, and the doctor's eyes widened. "I'm doing fine. The pain's just about gone, and I'm ready to go home, but do you know if the transplant worked?" Peter reached for another roll. "What? I'm hungry," Peter quipped when he saw the doctor's expression. "Would you eat that?" Peter asked, tilting his head toward the tray. "I didn't think so."

"Let me check your incision." The doctor pulled back the bedding to look at Peter's hip. "Looks very good," he commented. "As far as we know, the recipient has received the transplant, but it takes some time before we know if it was successful."

"Is there a way I can contact the recipient?"

"I'll pass on the message. If you don't have any other issues, it looks like we can have you out of here this afternoon." The doctor entered some information into his computer before saying goodbye and leaving the room.

"Are you going back to your house?" his dad asked. "I can stay there with you."

"I hadn't thought about it," Peter answered. He'd been too concerned with the procedure itself to worry about what would happen afterward, but he was going to need someone to help him at least for a while.

"I can stay with you, Peter, if you like," Russ said softly. "I don't want to intrude, though." Peter turned to his father, expecting him to be upset, but instead he saw him nod with a pleased smile on his face. Russ must have seen it too, because he took Peter's hand and held it.

"Don't you have to work getting the restaurant ready to open?"

"I've got the people hired, and Darryl is working with the servers at Café Belgie over the next few weeks. The initial kitchen staff are people Darryl and I already trust. The building is set up and ready. When he found out you were going to do this, he told me to take a few days off to make sure you were on the mend." Russ moved closer and lowered his voice. "Sometimes I think he and Billy can read minds, because they always seem to know what everyone needs before they ask."

"I've noticed that too. I think they're so happy together that they want the rest of the world to be as happy," Peter said before closing his eyes. Now that he was full, he felt tired and sort of dozed off. That was one of the things about being in the hospital—you could sleep when you wanted to and no one said anything about it.

THE doctor was true to his word, and that afternoon he stopped to check on him one last time. "Everything looks good, so we're going to let you go. I passed on your message through channels to the recipient of the transplant. I haven't gotten a response, but in these cases they often wish to say thank you, so don't be surprised if you hear from her."

"It's a woman, then," Peter commented. "Is she doing okay?"

"Yes, it's a woman, and that's all I know. It takes ten to twenty-eight days before we know if the marrow has grafted. So it could be some time." He signed some papers and handed them to the nurse, and just like that, Peter was sprung. After getting dressed, one of the orderlies helped him into his chair, and Russ carried the rest of his things as they exited the hospital. Russ drove him to his house and helped Peter inside and into bed.

"Can I get you anything? Are you hungry?" Russ offered, but Peter shook his head.

"Maybe later. There's something more important I'd like here with me, though." Peter patted the bed beside him, and Russ shook his head.

"I don't think you're up to bed company yet," Russ cautioned, backing away.

Peter rolled his eyes and held out his hand. Russ took it, and Peter guided him around and onto the bed. As soon as Russ lay down, Peter found a comfortable position and curled next to him. "I missed this."

"Me too," Russ sighed, and Peter felt him relax. "Do you realize that before you went into the hospital I'd stayed here with you more than I've been at Darryl and Billy's?"

"I noticed," Peter said, resting his head on Russ's shoulder. "I also noticed that I don't sleep as well when you're not here. Probably because I wish you were." Peter angled for a kiss, and Russ obliged, more than once. Peter let go of the discomfort and lost himself in Russ's kisses. Pretty soon he found himself moaning and hard, wishing Russ would move his hand from his shoulders to a place more fun.

"I know what you want, but I don't think that's a good idea yet," Russ cautioned. "But if you roll over carefully, I'll rub your back for you."

Peter agreed, and after another kiss, he slowly turned over, and Russ lowered the covers, his hands slowly moving over Peter's skin. A few times Russ let his hands wander over Peter's butt, and Peter heard himself moan when Russ did. "Just relax and don't get excited."

"Too late," Peter mumbled, and soon the smooth rhythm of Russ's touch and his soft humming had Peter's eyes closing and his breathing evening out, and before he realized it, he had fallen asleep.

He woke some time later. Russ wasn't in bed with him, but Peter could hear him moving in the house. "I brought you something to drink, and I'm making a light dinner."

"What time is it?" Peter asked through a yawn.

"Seven o'clock. You slept for most of the afternoon. How do you feel?" Russ moved close to the bed, setting the glass on a nightstand before leaning over him. Peter reached from under the covers, pulling Russ down for a kiss.

"Better, much better," he answered when Russ pulled up, but Peter tugged him down for another kiss. He'd missed Russ's touch, and he immediately deepened the kiss

"Do you really think this is a good idea?" Russ asked him, and Peter nodded. As far as he was concerned, it was a damned good idea, and it felt even better when Russ carefully climbed onto the bed with him.

"Yes, it's a brilliant idea," Peter mumbled as he got a taste of the skin near the base of Russ's neck. "I've missed you so much." Russ settled on the bed next to him, and Peter kept kissing and touching until Russ stilled his hands.

"I've missed you too, but you've just had surgery and you need to take it easy," Russ chastised gently. "I don't want anything to happen to you." Russ lay next to him, holding tight. Peter huffed softly, knowing Russ was right, but then he felt his lover's hands moving slowly over his skin, and his lips touched him ever so gently. "You have to lie there and promise me you'll tell me if anything hurts."

Peter nodded, and Russ slid down the bed. The covers slid away, and Peter lay naked and shaking. When Russ sucked on his nipples, Peter moaned and writhed on the bed, and when Russ kissed his way down Peter's stomach, the muscles fluttered with anticipation. Russ wrapped his fingers around Peter's cock, and his breath hitched, the firm grip sending shocks of pleasure up and down him. "Russ, please," he begged in a croaky voice.

"Do you promise to tell me if anything hurts?"

"God yes!" Peter cried, and Russ settled between his legs. Peter watched with rapt attention and body-shaking anticipation as Russ opened his mouth, sucking hard on Peter's cock. "Fuck," he groaned before he could stop himself. The searing hot wetness that surrounded him sent Peter to Nirvana. The stuff Russ did with his mouth and that little swirly thing he did with his tongue made Peter's eyes roll back in his head. "God," Peter moaned, and Russ slowly slid his lips down his length and then held still, swallowing around him. Russ had to stop himself from trying to move.

Peter felt his cock slip from Russ's lips, and small kisses peppered his stomach. "Do you know how special you are?" Russ asked, but Peter's eyes were glazed over and nearly all he could hear was his heart thrumming in his ears. "You gave of yourself so someone else could have a chance at a better life, someone you didn't even know." Russ brought his lips to Peter's, kissing him hard and breathtakingly deep. "You're an amazing man."

Russ kissed him once again and then took him deep. Peter could barely catch his breath as a wave of pleasure crashed over him. Every touch of Russ's hands and lips conveyed his love. How Russ did that, Peter had no idea, but he could feel it down deep.

Peter's eyes closed when Russ ran his tongue along his shaft, stroking him firmly with his hand, teasing that spot just below the head. He opened his mouth, ready to cry out, but no sound came as Russ made love to him. Each movement and touch conveyed his love more clearly than words ever could. Peter quickly felt the pressure build deep inside. Reaching down, he lightly placed his hands on Russ's hair, wanting a further connection with his lover. "Russ, I'm gonna come," he managed to croak out in warning, but Russ just sucked harder, intensifying his erotic assault, and Peter closed his eyes, letting his climax wash over him.

When he opened his eyes, Russ had shifted on the bed, lying next to him with a very satisfied smile on his face. When Peter smiled, Russ leaned close, kissing him deeply. Peter tasted himself on Russ's tongue, mixed with the slightly sweet flavor that he knew was unique to his Russ. *His.* Russ was his, he knew that now, and Peter wrapped his arms around Russ's neck, drawing him as close as he possibly could. "I love you," Peter said softly, his lips brushing Russ's as he said the words. "I truly and amazingly, completely, love you."

Russ didn't say anything, and Peter looked into his eyes and saw they were filled with tears.

"I thought I loved Barry, I really did. I was with him for four years and I really thought…." Russ blinked his eyes before rubbing them, a tear running down his cheek. "I was wrong. What I had with Barry wasn't love. I'm not sure what it was, but it wasn't that, because I know what real love is now and I have it with you." Russ hugged him, burying his face in Peter's shoulder. Peter could feel wetness on his skin, and he knew Russ was probably crying. Holding him, Peter cried as well for all the pain Russ had been through.

"I'm sorry," Russ said, lifting his head and brushing his eyes. "I'm not sure where all that came from."

"It's okay to cry when you're happy." Peter was truly happy, and Russ had made him so. Peter closed his eyes and felt himself falling back to sleep as he held Russ tight in his arms. This was how he wanted to feel for the rest of his life.

Their romantic moment was interrupted by a loud rumbling that was followed quickly by another. Russ began to laugh, and Peter felt mortified. "Was that you?" Russ asked, chuckling. "Damn, that was the loudest stomach rumble I've ever heard." Russ moved out of Peter's arms. "I guess that's my clue to finish making dinner." Russ stroked Peter's arm after getting out of bed. Peter shifted to the edge and began pulling his wheelchair closer. "Where do you think you're going?"

Peter paused. "I was getting up for dinner."

"I'll bring it in here for you." Russ leaned over the bed. "I intend to keep you in this bed for as long as I have to." Russ kissed him and then stepped back.

"I have to use the bathroom," Peter explained, and he let Russ help him into the chair. "I'll go right back to bed, I promise." Peter wheeled himself down the hall. "I hope you know I'm only doing this so I can attend practice with the team," Peter called before rolling into the bathroom, and all he heard was a growl in response.

IT TOOK him an additional day before his mother hen of a boyfriend would let him out of bed for anything but to use the bathroom. But today was Saturday, and Peter had nearly had a battle royal with Russ before he'd let him come to racing practice. It had almost been their first fight until Peter had promised that he'd take it easy. Russ had loaded his racing chair in the car for him, grumbling the entire time about "stubborn boyfriends not knowing what was best for them."

Peter transferred himself into the car before pushing his regular chair away from the car door so he could close it. Pressing the button, he raised the garage door and backed out of the garage, closing it again before heading over to the track.

The guys were all there and very happy to see him. "How did everything go?" Skip asked.

Peter told them the story, and then they began their warm-ups. For Peter, it felt great to be outdoors and moving again, the crisp morning air clearing out the cobwebs from the surgery. He took it easy, like he promised Russ, much to Skip's consternation, because in his words, "I've been looking forward to having you eat my dust." Once practice was over and Peter had assured everyone he would be more than ready for the competition in a few weeks, everyone headed home.

Peter felt restless and thought of going to the Acropolis to see how things were going, but he didn't want to disturb Russ at work. The restaurant was opening in a few weeks, and because of the interruption from his surgery, Russ had a lot still to do to make sure everything was ready. Reluctantly, he drove home. As he was pulling into the garage, his phone rang, and he answered it once he'd come to a stop and turned off the engine. "Hello," he answered tentatively when he saw the strange number on the display.

"Is this Peter?" a tentative female voice asked.

"Yes." Peter wondered for a second if this was a telemarketer.

"My name is Brenda Winters, and… I'm not sure how to go about this, but I received your marrow cells."

Peter felt a tingle of sheer electric excitement go up his spine. "How are you doing? I've asked my doctor a few times, but they hadn't heard."

"I just got results today," she sniffled, and Peter thought from her voice that she'd been crying. "My white blood cells have increased. It seems the transplanted cells have taken hold and are working. You saved my life." He heard what sounded like another sniffle, and then the phone rattled as though someone was taking it.

"Thank you, thank you, thank you!" a deep voice said into the phone. "Thank you for giving me back my Brenda. I can never repay you no matter how long I live." The man let out a whoop that nearly deafened Peter. The phone shifted again.

"Dean, honey, it's going to be fine," Brenda said with another sniffle as she came back on the phone, the celebratory yelling continuing in the background. "My doctor passed on your number, and I called to thank you for your kindness. If there's anything we can ever do to repay you…." Her voice drifted off, and Peter heard crying in the background. He felt like he was intruding on them, but at least they were tears of joy. "Would it be okay to call you again when we can actually talk?"

"Of course, I'm sure you have people you need to tell," Peter answered, and the line went silent.

Peter didn't remember setting down the phone or even driving, but he found himself outside the Acropolis, still in his car, with tears running down his cheeks. He'd never met Brenda, and he'd only had a five-minute phone call, but he was crying like a baby. He didn't even realize he was doing it until he heard a rap on the window.

"Peter, what's wrong?" Russ asked, reaching into the open window to take his hand. "What happened?"

Peter tried to take a deep breath and he faltered. It took another few minutes before he could talk. "Please help me inside," he managed to say, and Russ opened the back door and got out the racing chair. Peter slid into it, and Russ guided him toward the door. Once inside, Russ got him to a table and had someone bring him a glass of water. Peter gulped it while he tried to get his emotions under control. "I got a call from the woman who received the transplant," Peter gasped. "It took. She said her white blood cells are rising and that I saved her life." The tears began again, and he let them fall. This was the greatest feeling in the world—he'd actually saved someone's life. "She was crying, and her husband thanked me. It's a miracle." Russ wrapped his arms around Peter tightly, and Peter simply held him as his emotions ran rampant. Russ didn't say anything; he just hugged him for a long while.

Russ released his hug, still smiling as he took a glass of water. "Did she say her name?" Russ asked, gulping from the glass, and Peter drank from his, letting the ice water soothe his raw throat.

He hadn't been thinking too much about it, and at first it was difficult to remember. "Brenda, that's it—Brenda Winters." Peter set the glass on the table. He'd expected Russ to say something, but he was silent, and when Peter turned toward him, he saw the water slip from his fingers, the glass crashing to the floor. "What is it? Do you know her? She lives in Florida."

Russ reached for a chair and sat down, paying no attention to the mess. "Why in the hell can't I get away from him no matter what I do?"

"Who are you talking about?" Peter pushed back from the table, rolling to where Russ sat, being careful of the glass.

"Did she say anything else?" Russ asked as he stared at his shoes.

"I remember her calling her husband Dean," Peter answered, now becoming worried.

"Fuck." Russ looked as though he were going to be sick. "I can't get away from him no matter what." Russ took a deep breath and lifted his eyes. "Brenda Winters, with a husband named Dean, is Barry's sister." Peter sat speechless, staring. If he'd had a glass in his hand, he'd have dropped it too.

CHAPTER TEN

RUSS could barely move. Everywhere he turned lately, he seemed to run into some ghost of Barry. Thankfully he hadn't seen or heard from him since the bastard had been served the restraining order, but even today, he'd found bits of broken glass when they'd been setting up the server's station. It was an unpleasant reminder of the damage Barry had done. Russ still expected to see Barry behind every tree or in the bushes at night, and now this. Without thinking too much about it, because he knew he'd chicken out, Russ pulled out his phone and automatically dialed a number.

"Aren't you violating your own restraining order?" Barry asked snidely when he answered the phone.

"No. You can't have any contact with me, and I'm only calling to ask you a question. How's your sister?" He really wished he had Brenda's number with him so he wouldn't have to call Barry the Bastard, but he needed to know if what he thought was true.

"Why do you want to know?" Barry shot back.

"How's your sister, BB?" Russ asked again, raising his voice.

Russ heard Barry swallow. "Like you care, but she just got a transplant, and she called to say it seems successful," Barry explained. "Are you still dating that cripple?"

"Peter, or that cripple, as you call him, is the man who saved your sister's life!" That left Barry silent for a long time.

"I still…." Barry sounded a bit pathetic.

"That's enough, Barry. Thank you for the information."

"Russ, I still—"

Russ cut him off, and he found he didn't know what else to say, so he stared at the phone before closing the connection.

"Does it make you feel bad because I helped Barry's sister?" Peter asked.

"God, no." Russ stared at Peter, realizing he'd let his reaction to Barry color everything about which he should be happy. "I only met Brenda and Dean a few times, but they were always nice, and she's not like Barry at all. She's kind and considerate. She and Dean have had a tough time of it with her leukemia and the fact that they probably won't be able to have children even if Brenda recovers." Russ stood up and got a broom and mop to clean up the mess. "I know it doesn't sound rational, but I keep thinking he's still around and watching me all the time." Russ mopped up the water and then swept the glass into a dustpan before placing the shards in the trash.

"You know, there's no shame in finding someone you can talk to," Peter said. "I bet a lot of people who've been through what you have get those same kinds of feelings. Talking to a counselor might give you the tools to deal with them."

Russ didn't know what to think. What Peter was suggesting sounded so reasonable, especially in light of how he'd reacted to Brenda being the person Peter had helped. Her association with Barry was enough to set him off. "I'll think about it. I'm not sure how comfortable I am talking about this with strangers."

"I felt the same way after my accident, but Dad convinced me to give it a try, and I'll tell you, it helped me accept my limitations." Peter wheeled himself to where Russ was standing, taking his hand. "I was angry at the entire world. What had happened to me wasn't my fault, and I took it out on everyone and everything I could. Because of that, I wasn't progressing physically. Dad arranged for a psychologist to come see me, and at first I wouldn't talk to him, but once I started to open up a little, he was able to help me. I didn't need to see him for very long, but he really helped me and showed me I could be independent and have a good life again. I always thought it was the stuff you see in movies, but that's a bunch of crap. They're someone to talk to and they listen." Peter got a wild smile on his face. "It's either that, or you could take karate and beat the shit out of him if he gets close, but therapy's probably faster." Russ began to chuckle, and Peter joined along with him. "Give it some thought."

Russ could tell Peter definitely meant well, but he wasn't too sure. "I'll think about it." That was the most he felt he could promise. What he really wanted to do was smack Barry into the middle of next week.

"Russ, I'm not sure I'm getting the filling for the spanakopita right," Kevin, one of the cooks he was training, called from the kitchen door.

"I'll be right there," Russ told him, and he turned back to Peter. "I need to go, but thank you for telling me. After work we can celebrate, because saving someone's life is definitely worth celebrating." Russ tried to push away all thoughts of Barry and remember Brenda. She'd always been bright and full of life. Russ remembered her leukemia diagnosis a few months ago, and the last time he was in Florida with Barry, she hadn't been doing very well.

"I think that's a good idea." Peter gave him one of those smiles that told Russ they were going to be doing a lot more in the area of celebrating than just having a drink. Russ watched him go and then walked back into the kitchen.

Kevin was indeed having troubles with the filling, and Russ had him start over from scratch, the two of them working together. "Is he really your boyfriend?" Kevin asked as they worked through the recipe.

"Yes, why do you ask?" Russ stopped what he was doing.

"Nothing bad. My sister is in a chair, and it takes a special person to be with them. My sister wasn't as lucky as he is." Kevin returned his attention to his work.

"I'm the lucky one," Russ said softly before returning to his work. He continued working through and fine-tuning recipes and techniques well into the afternoon and early evening. Leaving the restaurant, he first headed to Billy and Darryl's, where the house had been taken over by Davey and Donnie, or at least it appeared that way. It had started raining sometime in the afternoon, so instead of playing in the backyard, they were building a fort in the living room.

"Come play cowboys with us," Donnie said as Russ spied their handiwork.

"I'd like to, boys, but I'm expected at Peter's house."

"Is he your boyfriend?" Davey asked as he stuck his head out of the stockade made of pillows.

"He is."

"Are you going to move in with him?" Donnie asked, and Russ realized he didn't have the answer to that question.

"Boys, wash so you can help with dinner. Uncle Darryl will be home in about an hour, and we're going to cook for him for a change," Billy instructed. The cowboy regiment herded itself upstairs, and footsteps echoed through the house as Billy walked to where Russ stood looking at the boys' fort. "You aren't staying?"

"No," Russ answered before going on to explain what had happened with the recipient of Peter's transplant, and who she was. "Needless to say, I was pretty freaked. I shouldn't have been, but I was."

"It sounds pretty shocking." The sounds of an argument drifted down the stairs. "I'd better break that up."

"I'm going to change clothes before I go," Russ said as he followed Billy upstairs. He got changed to the backdrop of two boys fighting over whose shirt was whose. Billy seemed to settle it, and when Russ came back downstairs, he saw that both boys were wearing identical blue-and-red-striped shirts. Russ didn't get it at all, but after saying goodbye and getting hugs from both boys and Billy, he headed over to Peter's.

The entire drive over, his mind kept wrestling with something Russ couldn't quite grasp. Something was just out of reach, but he couldn't put his finger on it.

Russ pulled into Peter's driveway and stopped, looking at the dark house. Something wasn't right. The front lights were on, but inside the house everything was dark. Russ automatically reached for his phone, ready to call the police, as his eyes scanned the neatly trimmed shrubs for someone lurking around. He didn't see anything, but that didn't mean someone wasn't there. Russ debated even getting out of the car at all. Besides, it didn't look as though Peter were home, even with the outside lights on. Deciding he was probably letting his imagination run away with him, Russ opened the car door and hurried up the walk, ringing the doorbell while he looked around constantly. The front door opened, startling Russ, and he nearly jumped into one of the flowerbeds. "I was beginning to think you weren't home."

It was then Russ noticed Peter's dress pants and shimmery silk shirt. Peter backed up, and Russ stepped inside. The house was indeed dark, but a soft glow came from the dining area. "What's going on?" Russ asked as he felt his nerves unwind, the realization that nothing was wrong sinking in. "Peter," Russ breathed softly as he followed Peter through the house, "you cooked for me." As a chef, Russ usually cooked for everyone else, so having someone cook for him was special.

"You said this was a celebration, so I wanted to make it a real one." Peter rolled to the refrigerator and opened the door, pulling out a bottle.

"When I saw everything was dark, I thought there might have been something wrong." The pop of the cork made Russ jump slightly.

"I didn't mean to scare you." Peter poured champagne into the glasses he'd set on the counter and handed one to Russ. "What should we drink to?" Peter asked, raising his glass.

"To the kindness of strangers," Russ offered.

Peter chuckled. "Which one of us is Blanche?"

Russ shook his head. He hadn't meant it that way, but it did sound rather Tennessee Williams. "Then to you, for demonstrating the kindness in your heart by giving the gift of life to a stranger." Russ knew it might have sounded corny, but it was true. After taking a sip from his glass, Russ leaned toward Peter and kissed him. He tasted like wine and spices, and Russ feasted on his lips as Peter moaned softly. "I can't believe you did this for me," Russ whispered against Peter's lips.

Peter set his glass on the counter. "Of course I did this for you. I love you." Peter pulled him into a kiss, and Russ nearly dropped his glass as he forgot about the wine he was holding in favor of the tingling lips on his. A soft ding sounded in the background, and Russ thought at first it might have been in his head, but Peter gentled the kiss and pulled away. "I don't want to burn dinner," Peter explained as he set his glass on the counter.

Russ backed away and let Peter work. Part of him wanted to help, but Peter didn't need it. He looked as at home in his kitchen as anyone Russ had seen. "Can I do anything?" he finally asked, feeling a bit useless.

"There's a salad in the refrigerator," Peter said as he leaned over the oven to remove what looked like a casserole dish. "It's nothing fancy. My mother used to make scalloped potatoes and ham when I was growing up, and I found her recipe the other day." Peter set the pan on one of the burners and closed the oven door. The aroma filled the kitchen with the scent of old-fashioned comfort food. Russ's stomach rumbled, and he opened the refrigerator door, removing a bowl of what looked like Caesar salad and setting it on the table. Then he carried the hot dish to the table, setting it on the trivet in the center.

Russ took his place and waited for Peter to approach the table. "This was very sweet of you."

"I have to confess I had an ulterior motive," Peter said as he filled their plates. "There's something I want to ask you, and…."

"You wanted to butter me up?" Russ offered.

"Sort of." Peter set down the spoon from the potatoes. "I want to ask you if you'd move in here with me." In the candlelight, Russ saw Peter bite his lip slightly and then reach for his glass. "You've spent most nights here with me, and when you're not, I miss you and wish you were here."

"Don't you think this is a little fast?" Russ asked, his nerves kicking up again as his doubts resurfaced. "It's not that I don't want to be with you, and I miss you when I'm not here, but this is a big step." Russ swallowed, watching as the candlelight reflected off Peter's eyes. "Are you sure this is what you want?" Russ wanted what he was feeling to be real so badly, and he knew the doubts he was feeling were coming from inside him and his own insecurities.

"Yes, I'm sure it's what I want, but what's important to me is what you want," Peter reassured him softly. "Don't let Barry make you doubt what you think will make you happy. If you want to get a place of your own, or continue living with Billy and Darryl, it won't affect the way I feel about you. I can promise you that."

Peter continued watching him, the reflection from the small flames dancing in Peter's eyes. He knew how he wanted to answer, so much it almost hurt. But he'd made such a mess of his life with Barry, could he trust his own judgment? Peter picked up his fork and began to eat, and Russ realized he was probably taking his silence for a no, or that his doubts were because of Peter being in a chair, and that wasn't the case at all. Russ wished he could be sure. Peter touched his hand lightly and smiled at him—he was patient enough and willing to wait.

"Yes," Russ said, jumping in with both feet. While his mind dithered, his heart made the decision, and as soon as he said the one simple word, it felt right. Like the last piece of a jigsaw puzzle that slides into its place, this felt perfect. The nerves, doubts, and indecision faded away and all he saw was Peter, his Peter.

There were arrangements to make and details to work out, but none of that mattered. When Peter took his hand before leaning over the corner of the table, everything but Peter faded away. The candle flames danced as Russ was kissed gently, but with such intense passion that he almost thought he was kissing one of the flames. They kissed again and again before settling back in their chairs, the food nearly forgotten.

Their stomachs reminded them rather forcefully. They talked of nothing, but it felt important, because at that moment everything seemed important and new because everything was a first. Their first meal together in what would become their home, the first time Russ did dishes in his new home, and the first time Russ led Peter back to what would become their bedroom. Russ carried the candles from the dining room, setting them on the dresser. "I want you to make love to me," Russ murmured in the flickering light once his lover had transferred himself to the bed.

Peter had shrugged, so Russ had rested on his side and let Peter lie next to him. How they made love didn't really matter. What was important to Russ was that Peter loved him, and Peter showed him just how much he was loved over and over again in ways more athletic than Russ would have thought possible. Their bodies connected, Peter buried deep inside him, Russ found himself brought to the edge time and time again with such patience that by the time Peter pushed him over the edge, Russ knew without a shadow of a doubt that not only had he made the right decision, he'd probably made one of the best decisions of his life.

"I love you," Peter told Russ as both of them came down from their body-wracking climaxes, their bodies still joined as one. Russ was completely content and happy. Turning his head to the side, they kissed, a little awkwardly, but happily.

Russ closed his eyes and held his breath as Peter slid from inside him. Russ felt Peter shift from behind him and then Russ was held again, Peter pressed to his back, a strong arm around his waist and a warm hand resting on his belly. "You're a special man, Russ." He shook his head, knowing that the truly special person on their bed was the one holding him. Peter didn't argue, but Russ felt Peter hold him tighter. Russ smiled to himself as Peter fell asleep, and he carefully got up and blew out the candles before climbing back into bed. Peter curled to him and mumbled something in his half sleep.

Russ stared at the ceiling, his mind refusing to settle. All day he'd been turning over in his mind how Barry's sister was Peter's bone marrow recipient. The odds of that were probably a million to one. "Holy shit!" Russ sat up in bed, and Peter bounced on the mattress next to him.

"What's wrong?" Peter mumbled from next to him.

"Sorry," Russ said, but he was now too excited to lie back down. "I just remembered something important. Barry's sister has been sick for a few months, and at one point, she had asked Barry to see if he was a candidate for a transplant, but his genetic markers or whatever they call them, weren't compatible with hers at all. That wasn't a surprise to Barry because Brenda was adopted." Russ heard Peter gasp. "And Barry's family comes from western Pennsylvania."

"Are you saying what I think you're saying?" Peter sounded stunned.

"It could be a coincidence, but it's possible. You have the genetic factors that make you a candidate for a transplant with her." Russ could feel himself shaking with excitement. "You need to talk to her and compare notes or get DNA tests. If Barry wasn't such a dick, we could ask him. I think I have her parents' number somewhere in my things, or I could look them up."

"No," Peter said from next to him, and Russ looked at his still half-asleep lover. "We won't involve anyone we don't have to. If we're wrong, there's no need to get a bunch of people upset." Peter pulled him back down on the mattress. "Go to sleep. There's nothing we can do tonight."

"How can you sleep?" Russ asked as he let Peter tug him into his arms.

"I don't know, but I can. Tomorrow morning will be early enough to see if your theory pans out. I've already hit a dead end on this once, so I'm not going to get my hopes up." Peter yawned, and Russ followed right behind him. "The attorney told me everything takes time, so while I agree this is promising and I appreciate you sharing your revelation with me, we should go to sleep." Peter rubbed

Russ's belly, and Russ closed his eyes. His mind still refused to settle, but he tried to keep his excitement to a minimum and eventually he managed to fall asleep. Still, he woke so many times he lost count, and eventually stared up at the ceiling, finally falling fast asleep just before he had to get up.

Getting out of bed when the alarm sounded, Russ shuffled into the bathroom. After shaving and taking a shower, he got dressed. Peter was stirring, and Russ made coffee, bringing his still sleepy lover a mug. "So, have you thought about how you want to go about seeing if Brenda is your sister?"

CHAPTER ELEVEN

PETER shook his head, chuckling almost to himself as he sipped from the mug. "I've only been awake for ten seconds." Peter took another sip and did his best to keep from burning his tongue on the hot liquid. "But I'll probably call the lawyer for advice. Maybe he can help." The last thing he wanted to do was get people spun up over nothing. He also made a mental note to call his dad. Peter tried to keep himself calm, but the more he thought about it, the more excited he became. His hand began to shake, and Russ took the mug before he spilled.

"So you are excited," he commented, and Peter smiled.

"Yeah. But I'm scared too. What if she isn't? I can't let myself get too hopeful," Peter cautioned, as much for himself as for Russ. Reaching for his chair, Peter got it into position and transferred himself into it. Russ kissed him goodbye and took both mugs into the kitchen. "Russ, would you put my racing chair in the car? I want to go to the track before work."

"Sure," Russ called from the kitchen, and as Peter got dressed, he heard Russ say goodbye and the back door close.

Peter hurried as much as he could and was on his way to the track in record time… for him, anyway. He spent half an hour warming up and then got going as fast as he could after making sure his hip was okay. The crisp morning air felt good, and as he worked, he let his mind mull possibilities. The thought of Russ moving in with

ANDREW GREY

him added to his excitement and energy, and Peter found his speed increasing. "Jesus," he heard someone say as he passed, and Peter slowed to see Skip sitting at the edge of the track in his chair. "You keep that up and there's no way I or anyone can beat you." He held his stopwatch so Peter could see it. "That's freakin' amazing."

"It was only a lap," Peter responded, keeping the pleasure at his time to himself.

"You do know that the regional competition is a qualifying event for the national Paralympic team? You could make it."

"No, thanks. I do this for fun. But if that's your goal, I'll help you train," Peter offered.

"If you don't want to reach the top, then why race?" Skip asked, already balancing on his back wheels.

"It helps me think. Besides, that's not where my priorities lie." Peter thought of Russ. "This is for fun."

Skip nodded, even though Peter figured he didn't really understand. "Do you really think you could help me go faster?" Skip lowered all his wheels to the ground.

"You could get a little more speed if you sat slightly differently in the chair. Lower your center of gravity and use more of your chest muscles to propel yourself." Peter demonstrated. "It's not much of a difference, but everything helps." Peter motioned toward the track. He and Skip took a few turns around, and while Skip beat him this time, Peter was right behind him, dang near a tie.

"Feels different," Skip told him as they coasted to a stop.

"It will because you aren't used to it, but in the long run it'll add speed. Give it a shot." Peter headed toward the side of the track. "I have to get cleaned up and go to work. But call if you want to train." Skip said he would, and Peter headed to his car, loading everything and then driving home. Peter cleaned up and changed before heading out to his first appointment, and by some miracle he actually arrived on time. The exercise had cleared his mind, and Peter was able to concentrate on his work—for now.

Somehow, Peter managed to make it through his morning appointments and not mess anything up. In fact, he got a number of good-sized orders that he called in to Annette before sending in the accompanying paperwork. By noon he was getting itchy, and since he was on the west side of his territory, he dropped in at the Acropolis and found Russ training his servers. "Hi, Peter," Russ called as he opened the door. "You're just in time. Have a seat and you can have lunch. Carl and Jenna will be our servers, and we're their practice customers. Jimmy is in the kitchen to prepare what we want, so can you stay for lunch?"

Peter laughed and rolled up to the table where Jenna set a place for him. She was polite and rattled off a bunch of imaginary specials before asking them what they would like to drink. Of course they got what Russ had already set up, but it was good practice. "Never ask the customer if they would like to keep their fork. If it's on the plate, take it and bring a fresh one. You never want to ask the customer anything you don't have to. They are here for a dining experience, and as servers you are to help and intrude as little as possible. Anticipate wherever you can. That's how you get top tips," Russ told both of them, and they left while he and Russ ate. "Would you please send Jimmy out?" Russ asked the servers before they disappeared into the kitchen, probably to let out a sigh of relief.

"Have you made any decisions?"

"Yes. I called the lawyer while I was in the car between clients, and he suggested I speak with Brenda. He said that the easiest way for both of us would be a simple DNA test. That would prove conclusively if we're related. So I was going to try calling her to see what she says, but since you already know her, I was sort of hoping you'd call to start the conversation."

Russ thought for a few minutes. "Okay. When we're done eating, we can call from the office," he said, and he continued eating until Jimmy joined them. "You did a good job on the moussaka. The spanakopita could be a little crispier, but that's the only issue I can find, and that's not bad. Good job!"

"Thanks, Russ." Jimmy beamed and then headed back into the kitchen. Peter returned to his food, tasting everything a second time. "Dad must have shared a lot of Mom's recipes, because this tastes like what I had growing up."

"He did. I had to adjust some of them for commercial preparation, but I think I got pretty close to the flavors your mother had." Russ continued tasting.

"You did," Peter assured him before cleaning the plate. "So when do you open? Have you set the official date?"

"We'll open for invitations-only a week from tonight, with a soft opening to the public two days later," Russ told him, and Peter could feel the excitement rolling off him. Once they were done eating, the servers returned to clear the plates and handed Russ the bill in the jacket, as they should. "You did very well," he told both of them as he stood up and led Peter back through the kitchen to the small office. Russ closed the door, and Peter showed Russ the number Brenda had called him on the day before. Russ dialed and they waited.

"Hello." Brenda's voice came through the speakerphone.

"Brenda, it's Russ. How are you doing?"

She sighed before speaking. "Well. I got a marrow transplant, and my white blood cells are up." Even Peter could tell she sounded tired.

"That's wonderful. I don't know if you've talked to Barry, but we're no longer together," Russ said diplomatically.

"It's about time. The way he treated you. I wanted to slap him more than once." Feisty—Peter liked her already.

"I have something I need to tell you, and it may come as a bit of a shock. The man who donated the marrow, he's my boyfriend. He helped me leave Barry." Russ had no idea how she would feel regardless of what she'd said earlier.

"I talked to him yesterday. Is that what you wanted to tell me?"

"No. Well, kind of. Brenda, Barry told me once that you were adopted, and I know you grew up in western Pennsylvania."

"Yes," she said, sounding suspicious.

"Brenda, I think there's the possibility that Peter, the bone marrow donor, might be your half-brother. His mother gave up a daughter for adoption in western Pennsylvania before she was married, and since his tissue was a match for yours…." Russ's voice trailed off, and Peter waited to hear her reaction.

"Oh my God," came through the connection, and Peter thought she might be crying. "I've been trying to find my mother for a while but never got anywhere." The sound of Brenda blowing her nose sounded through the speaker. "They put up so many roadblocks."

"I don't know for sure," Peter broke in, "but would you be willing to have a DNA test done to find out?"

"Yes." She was definitely crying now. "I'll ask my doctor about it."

"I'll do the same here," Peter said. "I hope we did the right thing by asking. I don't want you to get your hopes up, and I'm trying not to do the same thing." Peter had so much more he wanted to say to her, but he could tell Brenda seemed to be winding down. "Can we call you when I know something?"

"You'd better, and, Russ, don't you let my idiot brother get to you. You deserve to be happy, and if Peter makes you happy, I'm with you. Remember, I grew up with Barry, so I know better than anyone else that he can be a complete ass. So don't you worry about him."

"He was stalking me, Brenda," Russ said, and Peter held his hand.

"Doesn't surprise me. Barry never shared very well, and he certainly never liked to lose." Brenda's speech became slower, and Peter wondered if they should say goodbye, but she seemed determined. "This may sound unsisterly, but whenever we got together, it was you I looked forward to seeing, not him. So be happy,

Russ." The line got quiet for a few seconds. "They're here to poke and prod me some more. Goodbye for now." Brenda hung up, and Russ disconnected the speakerphone.

Peter stared at Russ, wondering what he was thinking after that surreal telephone call. Never in a million years had he expected the call to go like that, and for Brenda to be so supportive. "What's bothering you?"

Russ shook his head. "Nothing. I wasn't ready for that. I knew Barry wasn't close to his family, but for her to support me and to wish me to be happy without Barry…."

"She sounds like quite a lady," Peter said, secretly really hoping she was his sister and that he'd get the chance to know her better. He was finding it harder and harder not to get his hopes up.

"She is." Russ moved away from the desk, and Peter found the stuffing being hugged out of him. "Thank you."

"For what?" Peter asked with a confused smile.

"Everything," Russ told him before hugging again. "I wish I could spend the rest of the day with you, but I'll see you back at the house tonight." Russ touched Peter's chin, angling his head up before kissing him possessively. "I love you so very much."

"I love you too," Peter answered when Russ's lips slipped away from his. "I never gave up hope, but I never really thought I would find love, either." Russ ran his fingers through Peter's hair before kissing him again. When their lips parted, Peter could barely breathe, but Russ smiled at him, mouthing, "I'll see you tonight," and he left the room with a small wave.

Peter sat with a smile on his face and let his clouded mind clear before gliding out through the kitchen, saying goodbye to everyone before heading to his car.

The phone call still had him reeling a little, and once he was in the car, he allowed the hopeful excitement to wash over him. Less than two months ago, Peter hadn't even known he had a sister, and now, it was possible that he'd found her. Peter knew if he had found his sister that he was probably one of the luckiest people on the face of the earth. Starting the car, Peter pulled into traffic. On his way to his next appointment, Peter called his father to tell him what he'd found and to make sure he was okay. They hadn't talked much about him searching for his half-sister, and he didn't want to hurt him. It turned out he needn't have worried. His father was almost as excited as he was. "If you find her, it will be like getting a piece of your mother back."

"I talked to her today, Dad." Peter had already explained about the pieces that Russ had put together and how they'd led them to Brenda. "She's sick, but there's an energy inside her that's hard to describe."

"You would like her to be your sister, wouldn't you?" His dad really did sound pleased.

"Yeah, Dad, I would, but we won't know anything one way or the other for a while. We need to run tests to be sure."

"Pfft," his father scoffed. "You can wait for your tests, but in your heart you already know the answer. No matter what you want or what you might think, you already know. So go make your calls to the doctor and arrange for the tests, but your heart is already telling you the results."

Peter pulled up in front of his next client, a pizza place that over the years had become a regional institution, and Peter said goodbye and hung up the phone, mulling over what his father had told him.

FOOTSTEPS outside the door woke Peter from where he'd fallen asleep on the sofa, and he sat up as Russ came in the front door. "I wasn't expecting you to work so late," Peter said around a yawn.

"I wasn't expecting to be this late, either, but Darryl needed help, so I chipped in," Russ explained as he strode to where Peter was sitting, kissing him hard. "So how did everything go?" Russ sat next to him, holding him.

"I called the doctor, and he had me stop in and they swabbed me. He ordered the DNA profile, and they can use it to compare to Brenda's when she gets hers done." Peter leaned his head against Russ's shoulder.

"I bet you're excited," Russ commented gently, and Peter tilted his face toward Russ's.

"I am, and I think it's time for bed so I can show you just how excited I am." Russ looked at him blankly for a split second and then smiled. "I've been lying here for a while thinking about you and how good your hands and dick are going to feel while you're fucking me." Peter didn't usually talk like that, and it felt both naughty and hot, especially when this time as Russ kissed him, Peter felt Russ's hand slide over the bulge in his pants.

Russ stood up, and Peter transferred to his chair and hastily rolled to the bedroom. He didn't even turn on the light as he got on the bed and began stripping off his clothes. By the time Peter was naked, Russ was already in bed with him, his hands doing everything Peter had imagined and more. "We should get tested," Russ murmured softly into Peter's ear. "That way I can be inside you, skin to skin."

The thought made Peter tremble slightly, and when Russ skimmed his fingers over his opening, Peter groaned and moved back into the touch. "Russ, don't wait." Peter heard Russ hiss when he realized Peter was already lubed and ready.

"You have been waiting for me, haven't you?" Russ asked, and he slid a finger, long and thick, into Peter's body. Peter growled loud and long, letting Russ know he was not feeling particularly patient. Russ added a second finger, scissoring them, scraping over the spot inside, pulling another groan from deep within Peter's chest.

"Yes!" Peter answered with a cry, wishing Russ would hurry up.

Russ smoothed his hand down Peter's side, and Peter pushed back against him, feeling greedy as hell. Peter knew Russ was trying to slow things down, but he was having none of it. The last few hours had felt like foreplay, and he was ready and aching. A rip behind him had Peter holding his breath, and he felt Russ moving and then his lover's cock pressed to his opening. "Peter?" Russ asked before pressing forward.

"I won't break," Peter growled, and Russ surged forward, driving into him. "Yeah!"

"Pushy bottom, aren't you?" Russ commented from behind him, and Peter nodded as he felt Russ pull away.

"Pushy gets what he wants," Peter answered, his voice trailing off into a moan as Russ drove back into him. Peter held onto the edge of the mattress. Russ slid his warm hands over his stomach, and then Peter felt hot, searing hands wrap around his dick. Russ didn't stroke, he simply held him tight in his fist, fucking Peter as though the world were coming to an end.

"I love you, Peter," Russ chanted in his ear. "You are fucking amazing, and I'm not going to stop until you feel it for the next week!" Russ's deep, raspy voice stoked Peter's desire as much as the world-class fucking Russ was giving him.

"I love you too, Russ, now fuck me like you mean it!"

Russ thrust hard, snapping his hips, until he was buried deep in Peter's body. "I'm going to… have to… wash your mouth out… with soap." Russ punctuated his words with deep, hard, driving thrusts that shook the bed and Peter's vision.

"Fuck first… wash mouth later." Peter gave up on talking and held on for what was undoubtedly the ride of his life. Peter barely realized Russ was stroking him until his orgasm crashed into him and he came, his eyes clamped shut, mouth hanging open, the pressure in Peter's head near explosive levels, not that he minded or cared.

The post-orgasmic haze cleared, and Peter rested on his side, Russ still deep inside him. Soothing words flowed over him, and Peter turned his head. The kiss was sloppy at best, but he didn't care, and Peter figured Russ didn't, either. "You're full of surprises," Russ said as he sucked on Peter's ear. Peter nodded slowly and made happy, contented noises, but talking took too much energy. Peter gasped when Russ slipped from inside him, then slowly rolled over to face his lover, who was disposing of things.

"So are you," Peter responded, wrapping his arms around Russ once he settled on the bed again. "I never thought a man like you would ever fall for me." Russ pulled him close.

"The only reason it took so long for you to find someone is because you were waiting for me," Russ said before moving closer. "So don't lament the journey, because it led you to me." Russ moved closer, and Peter felt a leg work between his as Russ pressed him back onto the mattress, kissing him languidly. Peter tried to come up with something clever to say, but gave up, because clever was not high on the list of priorities at that particular moment.

EPILOGUE

PETER hated winter—propelling his chair through snow, wet wheelchair treads. He would be more than happy once spring arrived, and hopefully that would be any day now. It had actually been nice for a few days, until it started snowing again. Pushing open the door to the Acropolis, Peter grumbled as one of his wheels slipped on slush and he had to shift his weight to keep from sliding. Why Russ had asked him to come down after work on a day like this was beyond him. He had just wanted to go home and wait for Russ to join him.

Once inside, he looked around and saw the group of wheelchair racers gathered around one of the tables. "Hey, guys," he called and glided over, the foul mood he'd been in immediately beginning to lift. "What's going on?" After the restaurant's opening about six months ago, the Acropolis had quickly become the hangout for the wheelchair racers, so it really didn't surprise Peter that they were here. Almost every evening part or all of the team seemed to be there. It wasn't anything formal, but it just seemed to work out that way.

"We tried calling, but we just got voice mail," Skip explained as he backed away from the table with a grin on his face.

"You heard," Peter said, and Skip's smile got larger.

"I made the team, and I'm going to the Paralympics in London this summer. But I need someone to go with me for moral support." Skip looked at him, and Peter in turn looked at the other guys.

"Me? You want me to go with you?"

"Yeah. You've been working with me for months, and I'm faster and have more control than ever," Skip said, still grinning. "I couldn't do this without you, man. Together we can't lose." One of the side benefits of working together was that as Skip had gotten faster, he talked less about winning and actually put more of his energy into his racing. He was unstoppable, and along the way Peter had discovered a talent for coaching he hadn't known he had.

Russ came out of the kitchen, and Peter looked at him, wondering if he knew. He did, if his smile was any indication. "I already called Darryl, and if you want to go, we can go. He said they'll help fill in here, as long as we do the same when he and Billy go on vacation."

"Cool, we're in." Peter reached over the table and high-fived Skip. "Is that why you called me down here?"

"Sort of," Russ answered. "Actually more of a happy coincidence than anything else." Russ held up a finger before disappearing back into the kitchen. Peter wondered what was going on and looked at the other guys, who all shrugged. Then Russ came back through the door with two people following behind him. "They wanted to surprise you."

Peter gasped and swallowed hard as a woman who looked amazingly like his mother walked toward him. "Brenda? Oh my God." He glided over to her, and they looked at each other, staring across what seemed like years to Peter. She bent down slowly and hugged him. Peter returned it, and as simple as that, he had a sister. Up till then, she was more an abstract idea than anything else, but now she was real. "I've wanted to see you for so long," he said as he cried onto her shoulder, realizing she was doing the same thing.

"Me too," she said as she slowly stood back up. "The doctors didn't want me traveling."

Peter knew she couldn't travel. He'd offered to come down to meet her, but with all the immune-suppressive drugs she'd been on, that wasn't a good idea, either. When he'd talked to her last, she had said they were hopeful she could travel this summer.

"The doctors gave her permission to travel last week, and she had me booking the plane tickets as soon as she got off the phone," Dean explained before Brenda squealed and hugged him once again, tears flowing for both of them. "She's been like that for days," Dean added with a smile.

Peter motioned toward an empty table and followed Brenda. Peter took the place next to her, and they began to talk. A lot of what they asked, they'd already talked about on the phone, but it seemed more important face to face. "I framed the pictures you sent," Brenda told him at one point. Peter had sent her pictures of himself and Russ, along with pictures of their mother. She'd called him when the pictures arrived, and they'd both cried over the phone.

"I did the same. The picture of you and Dean hangs in our hallway." He didn't add that it was with the rest of the family pictures because it wasn't necessary. They both knew what the other meant.

Plates of food were placed on the table by one of the servers, and both of them munched absently as they talked and talked. After all, they each had an entire lifetime to catch up on, and they both seemed to feel the need to say everything there was to say while they had the chance to say it. At one point they seemed to realize that both Dean and Russ had disappeared somewhere, but they continued talking, only stopping when the guys said goodbye, until Peter saw that Brenda was getting tired. She was so much like his mother Peter could barely get over it.

Carefully, Brenda stood up. Dean seemed to appear at her side. "Getting tired?"

"Yes," she answered with a slight nod of her head. Just like Peter's mother.

"Where are you staying?" Peter asked.

"Russ helped us arrange for a hotel in town. He also said we were to come to your house for breakfast in the morning," Brenda explained, and Peter looked at his lover, not sure if he should be pleased or mad at him for knowing and not saying a word. Brenda hugged him again, and Dean shook his hand before they said goodbye.

"You know you're in trouble for keeping this a secret," Peter told Russ once they'd gone.

"She asked me to, and even though they booked the tickets, they weren't sure they could come until the last minute," Russ explained quietly, since they were in the dining room.

"That doesn't let you off the hook," Peter scolded.

"I'll apologize properly when we get home. I promise," Russ told him softly, and Peter nodded.

"How long will that be?" Peter asked as he shrugged on his coat and headed toward the door.

His chair stopped, and Russ leaned over the back. "I'll be right behind you." Peter had no doubt about that.

ANDREW GREY grew up in western Michigan with a father who loved to tell stories and a mother who loved to read them. Since then he has lived throughout the country and traveled throughout the world. He has a master's degree from the University of Wisconsin-Milwaukee and works in information systems for a large corporation. Andrew's hobbies include collecting antiques, gardening, and leaving his dirty dishes anywhere but in the sink (particularly when writing). He considers himself blessed with an accepting family, fantastic friends, and the world's most supportive and loving partner. Andrew currently lives in beautiful historic Carlisle, Pennsylvania.

Visit Andrew's web site at http://www.andrewgreybooks.com and blog at http://andrewgreybooks.livejournal.com/. E-mail him at andrewgrey@com cast.net.

The Taste of Love stories by ANDREW GREY

A TASTE OF *Love*

ANDREW GREY

http://www.dreamspinnerpress.com

A SERVING OF Love

ANDREW GREY

http://www.dreamspinnerpress.com

Also by ANDREW GREY

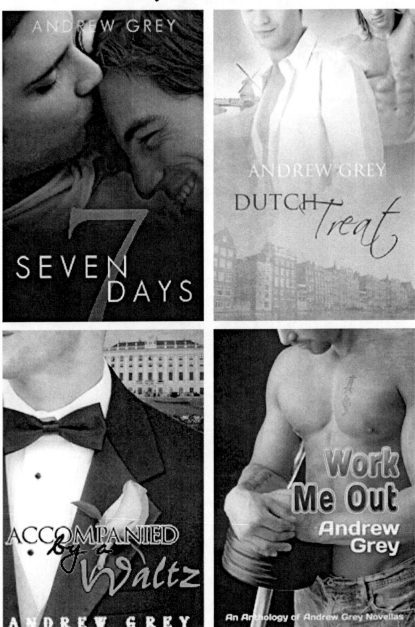

http://www.dreamspinnerpress.com

The LOVE MEANS… stories

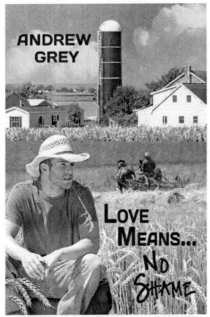

http://www.dreamspinnerpress.com

The BOTTLED UP stories

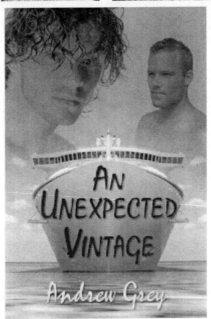

http://www.dreamspinnerpress.com

The ART stories

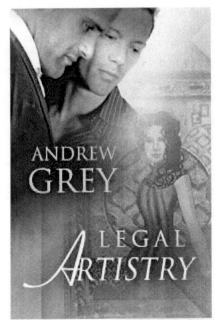

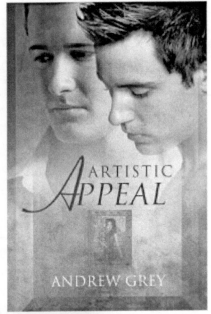

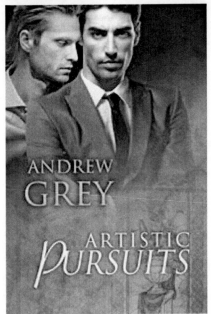

http://www.dreamspinnerpress.com

The RANGE stories

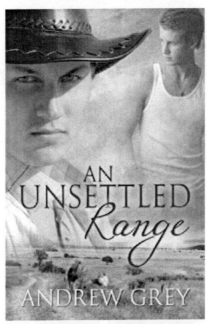

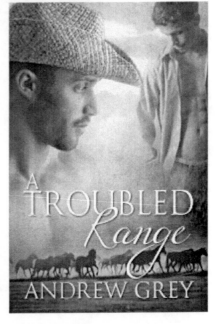

Contemporary Fantasy by ANDREW GREY

http://www.dreamspinnerpress.com

CPSIA information can be obtained at www.ICGtesting.com
Printed in the USA
LVOW090141160512

281869LV00006B/40/P